Caroline,
With best wishes,
3. xi. 98

THE RIVER CROSSING

Peter Rippon

MINERVA PRESS

ATLANTA LONDON SYDNEY

THE RIVER CROSSING
Copyright © Peter Rippon 1998

ISBN 0 75410 418 4

First Published 1998 by
MINERVA PRESS
195 Knightsbridge
London SW7 1RE

Printed in Great Britain for Minerva Press

THE RIVER CROSSING

To Angela, and all her kind

Acknowledgements

From *The Ascent of Man* by Dr J. Bronowski,
published by BBC Publications

From *Into the Heart of Borneo* by Redmond O'Hanlon
reprinted by permission of the
Peters Fraser & Dunlop Group Ltd

Cover design from an original watercolour
by Daniel Mason

'Get some jungle boots, good thick trousers and strong shirts,' said the Major. 'You won't want to nancy about in shorts once the first leech has had a go at you, believe me. Acclimatise slowly. The tropics take people in different ways. Fit young men may pass out top here and then just collapse in Brunei. You'll think it's the end of the world. You can't breathe. You can't move. Then after two weeks you'll be used to it. And once in the jungle proper you'll never want to come out.'

Redmond O'Hanlon
Into the Heart of Borneo

Prologue

UNTIMELY
DISAPPEARANCE OF
LADY EXPLORER

Despite extensive enquiries conducted by Her
Majesty's Diplomatic Corps on behalf of Mr
Theophilus Tew of Leamington Spa, there is still no
news from Tehran of the fate of Miss Eleanor Tew,
formerly of Clough Hall, Cambridge. Miss Tew, the
well-known authoress of *Bavarian Journal* and *A
Pyrenean Excursion*, both successful titles published by
Messrs Chatto & Windus in their popular 'Books for
Travellers' series, is known to have struck out into
the fastness of the Bakhtiari Mountains of south-west
Persia with the intention of making contact with the
nomadic peoples of that region. From her regular
correspondence both with her father, Mr Tew, and
Miss Anna Rowlandson, her friend of Cambridge
years, it is known that Miss Tew did indeed achieve
this aim and did set out as originally intended to observe the cycle of the nomadic year in the company
of the native tribesmen of the locality. Of late, however, the continuing absence of correspondence from
this venturesome lady has given rise to fears that
something untoward may have transpired to put her
life at risk, if not indeed to end it. Hence the anxieties

of Mr Tew who, interviewed recently at his home in Leamington Spa, gave expression to those very real concerns for the well-being of his eldest daughter which have led him to initiate the aforementioned as yet fruitless enquiries.

The Times newspaper
September 1882

Part One

Eleanor Tew

Chapter One

The little girl turned from the nursery window, where she had been watching the rain as it drifted in rippling sheets across the private dell to the rear of the fine Regency house where she lived.

'When is it going to be my turn?'

One of her brothers, four years her elder at the age of twelve and to her view therefore quite enormous, looked down upon her from the rocking horse where, a dashing Cherry Picker, he had been about to cut down his twin, a hapless Cossack.

'Willie's next. I'm the Lancer now, he's the Russian. Then we change round. You can come after that. Anyway, girls don't ride properly because they can't.'

'Oh yes, they can. Because they do, in remote parts of the world.'

The Cossack got up from where he had been cowering from the onslaught of the Lancer.

'What does she mean – remote? What's that?'

'It's where savages and heathens live. Faraway.'

'So, what has that to do with us? We're English. The best.'

'Not when we don't know perfectly ordinary words, we're not.'

'Oh, be quiet, Eleanor. You're only a little girl.'

'Not too little to put you back where you belong, William!'

Taking advantage of his unbalanced position, she pushed him hard, back onto the nursery floor.

'Eleanor, that's naughty!'

She turned to Frederick, disdaining the horseback reprimand.

'Is that all you can say? I thought you were supposed to be soldiers. Real soldiers fight, they don't waste time complaining. That's it! I'll fight you for a ride, if you dare!'

At this point William, goaded beyond forbearance, swept her feet from under her from where she had pushed him to the floor as Frederick, dismounting, attacked simultaneously. Kicking, struggling and punching, she was ejected from the room and put out onto the landing despite a surprisingly energetic resistance.

'You shall stay out of the nursery until you learn to be a good girl and leave us our horse!'

'He's my horse, too! He's my Bucephalus as much as he is yours!'

Although she was so much smaller and lighter than they, the twins found her difficult to subdue, for Eleanor fought with intelligence and knew that kicked kneecaps and ankles hurt and that wrists, nipped or bitten, cause hands to lose their grip. They were all three having a marvellous time that wet afternoon until the heavy crash of pottery breaking brought an abrupt end to the fracas.

'The jardinière!' said Frederick.

'Oh, lor!' said William.

From below a door latch clicked, the sound clearly audible in the stairwell.

'Now we've done it,' said Eleanor.

'And what, pray, have you done?' said a voice like thunder, as its owner began to mount the stairs.

'Father!' whispered William, appalled.

'Stand your ground, sir!' said Frederick sharply. 'And if we're beaten, no tears, d'you hear me?'

'I shall stand with you,' said Eleanor. 'I started it.'

'You're a brave girl,' said Frederick. 'And you can't half fight!'

'Not half,' said William.

'Now, gentlemen,' said the voice of doom, as the formidable figure of Theophilus Tew made its appearance at the top of the stairway, 'account for yourselves, if you please!'

Retribution, summary and painful, was meted out to the boys. Eleanor escaped the beating but had to endure the reprimand from her beloved father. That night the three went to bed supperless but not without a certain equanimity, for the incident had taught them something they were not to forget about the nature of the bond among them.

★

That night too Eleanor dreamed her particular dream, which began, as it invariably did, with her semi-conscious contemplation of the flowery patterns of the wallpaper by her bed. As she dozed off into sleep, these would assume the outlines and contours of a landscape, melting into a dream vision of high and lonely places, of a mountainous terrain against which there moved, across swift-flowing, icy rivers and over formidable gradients of scree and similar rocky wastes, a concatenation of figures both animal and human. They moved apparently raggedly yet clearly with some kind of collective purpose in mind, and their clothing and such accoutrements as they carried with them were outlandish, primitive, not of Europe or of modern times.

But the strangest thing about this dream to Eleanor, amid the opulence and comforts of her Leamington Spa home, was the recognisable familiarity of it all: a landscape where eagles hovered high over wild hillsides flecked bright with gladiolus and gentian, and of the travelling people and the animals they herded with them. And with all of this there went, by way of addition, the sense of an indescribable contentment and happiness, of an identity established, confirmed and acknowledged and having to do with a notion of belonging such as Eleanor at home experienced only with her father, Theophilus Tew, that top-hatted, side-whiskered, cigar-smoking Brunel of a man, and certainly never with her mother or even, much as she loved them, her twin brothers or, later, with one or two exceptions, her Cambridge contemporaries, gilded protégées of an early generation of Miss Ann Jemima Clough's lady scholars.

★

At the time of the birth of his third child and first daughter, Eleanor, Theophilus Tew, of Clarendon Crescent, Leamington Spa, was at the height of his professional life as an engineer, with certain vital responsibilities with regard to sewage, water supply, roads and bridges in the prosperous Warwickshire borough in which he resided. It was typical of the man, gentleman that he was, to recognise the essential character of the services for which he was responsible, which concerned the health and well-being of the populace in general, and that effectively from the gentry of the county or the great Lord Broke in his castle at Warwick to the meanest, raggedest errand boy domiciled in his family's tiny cottage in one of the new streets behind the parish church.

Theophilus Tew was a mathematician who took a pride in tap water, who loved the logical design of a functioning machine as well as the ingenious and economical organisation of a fowl's internal parts. He was a man with an unshakeable sense of his own self, of his duty to science and the public good, and his first girl-child, who was to become his beloved Eleanor, followed her rumbustious brothers, the twins Frederick and William, into the world in the year following the Great Exhibition of 1851.

Over the space of the next few years three more daughters, Rachel, Gwendolen and Jemima, were born to Theophilus and Charlotte Tew, until by 1862 the family was firmly established in its final form, the boys thriving at Rugby School and the girls being educated privately at home by a cherished governess. Only Eleanor, who, by the age of scarcely ten, had shown such an aptitude for the study of mathematics, was excused certain hours with Miss Beaufoy in order that these might be spent with her father, who tutored her himself.

Frequently at evening time, over claret or brandy and hot water and a cigar or two, Theophilus Tew would discuss his favourite daughter with her godfather, his medical friend, Doctor Samuel Barnes.

'You know, Barnes, the world has too little use for one such as Eleanor. I mean, who ever heard of a lady mathematician? And yet, the child is a mathematician, as her brothers could never be, not in a thousand years.'

'Then this is the world's loss, is it not, Tew? And, indeed, who ever heard of a lady physician?'

'A certain Miss Nightingale acquitted herself rather creditably, did she not, at Scutari?'

'She most certainly did. And quite right too. Ladies such as these need more space, Tew, and it must be created for them. For as things are, we waste much that is of value in the female intelligence by the way we conventionally constrain them in domesticity and motherhood.'

'What a fine thing it would be, Barnes, if Eleanor could, say, read mathematics at Cambridge! There is talk, you know, of a college for ladies, movements afoot, that kind of thing.'

'I am aware of that, Tew. The thought had crossed my mind too.'

'What a good fellow you are, Barnes. So. We shall have to see, shall we not? Now that Frederick and William seem set upon the army, and I see no reason why they should not both go that way provided their tutors are agreeable... The other girls are too little to concern me as yet, but Eleanor does. She will require guidance and counsel.'

'And she shall have it, of course. For it would be a fine thing, would it not, to blaze a trail?'

'It would, my dear doctor. Truly it would.'

★

Even as she came to leave it for a room of her own, Eleanor Tew loved the nursery: she loved the warmth, the starched cleanliness, the scents and odours of the little girls, her sisters, around whom there bustled a capable nanny who was not so much older than they, for all her responsibilities, that she could not enjoy pillow fights, tumbles and the shrieks of wild laughter that go with the privileges of security, contentment and good food. For, despite the admonitions of a mother increasingly enfeebled by a temperament ill equipped to cope with the energetic young life to which she had given birth, the Tew household bore the stamp of Theophilus and celebrated, through its distinctive style, a forceful independence of mind and a blithe, at times almost contemptuous, disregard of the more stifling conventions of the day. For Theophilus's formative years had been the Regency years, and there was about him a characteristic, almost raffish touch of the eighteenth century, which he impressed even as he breathed upon the ethos of his home. Charlotte, by contrast, seemed simply to fade into ethereality with the passing of the years, finding sanctuary at last in a religious introspection which was to become increasingly stultifying as she aged.

Eleanor grew up tall, strong and energetic, a slender, fair young woman with her father's features, a composed smile and a cool, incisive intellect, instantly to be discerned from the steady, enquiring appraisal of a penetrating gaze of the kind which did not invariably commend itself to her elders – these often in the form of her brothers' army friends.

'Sharp sort of girl, your sister, Tew, what? Bit too bright for comfort, if you ask me.'

For Fred and Willie, free at last from the constraints of Rugby, grandly accoutred in fine military attire, still as rumbustious as ten, even fifteen years previously, moved through society lavishly provided with friends of similar disposition and with never a single thought of a kind to trouble a sound constitution and a fatalistic insouciance of the cheeriest order. Moustachioed and pomaded, the twins Fred and Willie danced, gambled, dined, flirted, rode, drank and partied.

It was on one such social occasion, instigated at Clarendon Crescent by the twins, that Eleanor made the acquaintance of an officer of rather a different kind.

Nicholas Duvivier, some ten years older than his twin subaltern friends, was a captain of thirty, a handsome veteran of Balaclava scarred by what had quite clearly been a ferocious sabre cut across the face. He was a quiet man, a traveller, linguist and cartographer, whose grave, gentlemanly dignity immediately endeared him to the Tew parents and to those of their friends who made his acquaintance during the course of his brief visit, although, in one or two of these latter, the uncompromising reminder of the grimmer realities of military life which he wore so stoically across his features did give rise to some aversion, repugnance even. Then it was that Theophilus, in characteristic style, found himself obliged to make clear in no uncertain terms that the reality of soldiering lay somewhat beyond the colourful garb and the kind of roistering social life which appeared as yet to constitute army life for his own sons. And, whilst he was wise enough to realise that neither of them had it in him to emulate their older friend, however much they hero-worshipped him and completely mis-understood him, he was grateful for the circumstance which had caused him to befriend the boys, and hoped that they might learn something from him.

'Dashed fine swordsman, Duvivier, Father. You should see him, sir.'

Theophilus decided for the moment to put his hopes to one side, and smiled to himself at the language of the mess so casually and confidently imported into the den, his private domain, where he was sharing a jug of claret with his sons.

'I'm quite prepared to believe you, William.'

'Can't think what he sees in Eleanor, though, can you? I mean, she's scarcely out of the nursery and the feller's always talkin' to her.'

'Perhaps she questions him, Frederick, on things he likes to talk about?'

'Gentlemanly feller, Duvivier, to show that kind of patience towards a little sister. And what can she want to know, anyway, of those outlandish languages he speaks? Extraordinary noises the man can make, what, Will? Really quite extraordinary!'

'Well, given that Miss Beaufoy did a rather better job on Eleanor's French and Latin than Rugby did on yours, gentlemen, if I may say so, perhaps your sister might just have found it in her to wish to explore something slightly more exotic, don't you think?'

'Oh certainly, Father. If you say so. Absolutely.'

'Can't see why a girl of her age – or of any age – should want to do that, if I may say so, sir.'

Theophilus, on the point of giving up, made one more effort prior to retreating into the kind of affectionate forbearance he had long since learned to entertain towards the twins.

'Well, Frederick. Perhaps you might consider that there are people who are fascinated by what is strange, unfamiliar, different even to the point of outlandishness. You said just now, sir, that Captain Duvivier can utter extraordinary sounds, did you not? What can they add up to, these sounds, if not something as familiar and mundane in its way as the English we are now speaking to each other? Perhaps there may be fascination to be had from fathoming how this may be. Do you see, my boy?'

'Frankly, sir, not exactly. But perhaps something to the point.'

'And you're sayin', are you, Father, that Eleanor thinks like that?'

'Yes, William.' Theophilus smiled at his sons. 'Most certainly she does.'

'What an extraordinary thing! I mean, little El!'

The look of bewilderment in William's eyes as he struggled to comprehend was something which had endeared him to his father since the days when, a little boy and the junior twin, he had striven so anxiously to keep pace with his brother. Theophilus sipped at his wine and privately relished the irony of himself, aged fifty something, feeling protective of his muscular, military sons. For indeed, he mused, and not without satisfaction, they had little need of him now, secure as they were within the haven of an established hierarchy and under the tutelage of such as Nicholas Duvivier. A complex, restless man, Theophilus surmised, a man searching for some kind of purpose to the scheme of things and finding nothing beyond a dazzling complexity, a dim sense of all that is marvellous and much that is unfathomed. And indeed, he mused, in the wake of Darwin's recent book there had developed amongst thinking men a new boldness, a kind of assurance about the whole business of enquiry, of curiosity which might be seen to have evolved from the circumstances of the book's publication some eight years ago and the furore it had aroused. Certainly, the man Wilberforce had done the Church no credit by the signal failure of his attempt to discredit Darwin in the notorious Oxford debate at the Pitt-Rivers with Huxley. And if the world were changing thus, the process must surely result in more rather than less space for Eleanor and her kind, for Duvivier and his. Thus, deep in the very heartland of middle-class Victorian respectability, Theophilus Tew savoured his claret and pondered the real possibility, as it seemed, of a new age of intellect, following on from the empirical curiosities of certain French philosophers of the previous century. There was a sense in which the Revolution in France, for all its horrors and atrocities, had enabled that nation to establish a truly republican slant on things, with the Church there properly relegated to the confines of its own sphere. In England the sway of Wilberforce and his ilk was too great for the good of enquiry and intellect, despite the forceful movements now emerging. It would take time, Theophilus mused, and a very great deal of it most likely, before the stranglehold of institutionalised religion, shored and buttressed by the weight of monarchy and society, could be induced or even compelled to release the mind of England from timidity and torpor. And here Theophilus gave thanks to whatever gods of circumstance there might be for having conferred upon him the incontrovertible social pre-eminence of Norman French ancestry through his mother's line, and, with it, the room for manoeuvre independent of the odious conventional constraints of the moment. And what a world was out there!

He recalled his studies in Germany, his travels in the Balkans and later in Scandinavia, the latter at the invitation of a Swedish count befriended in Vienna. The castle at Skokloster, for instance, an exquisite gem of northern baroque viewed from across the reaches of Lake Mälaren against a background of pine forest; the wastes of the far north, with the nomadic Lapps and their reindeer. What an enterprise, to put your own girdle round about the earth! He and Barnes, perhaps, one day? Regrettably not Charlotte who, now a faded shadow of her marvellous self of twenty years previously, had chosen to immure herself in fashionable superstition of the most benighted kind and was in consequence no longer a marriage partner in any real sense of the word... Theophilus, as he had schooled himself to do, put futile regret out of his mind and brought his thoughts back to the present. Eleanor, most certainly, should study and travel. And for all that he genuinely loved each and every one of his children, he had to acknowledge that what was to become of Eleanor was what concerned him most nearly. For Eleanor mattered in some way the others simply did not. They would thrive, he knew, with his fortune behind them; they would go their various ways almost inevitably, barring the untoward – and he thought briefly of Montaigne's admonition in regard to a parent's love of his children, who could so easily and did so frequently die, despite, nowadays, the ministrations of Barnes and his medical kind.

'Sir?'

Theophilus came round, blinking.

'I beg your pardon, my boy. I was lost in my thoughts.'

'May I give you some wine, Father?'

'Thank you, Frederick. Then finish the jug, you fellows, if you will, and get Selden to decant another bottle, would you, for Doctor Barnes when he arrives.'

'I say, Father.'

'Yes, William?'

'Don't you think, sir, that we might perhaps rescue Duvivier from the ladies? The feller's missin' out on your fine claret, Father.'

Theophilus smiled at his son's solicitude for the privations of his guest.

'Certainly, William. But be polite to Miss Beaufoy, sir, and gentle to your sister.'

'Oh, absolutely, Father.'

'And, William?'

'Yes, sir?'

'Perhaps Captain Duvivier might care to join Doctor Barnes and myself for a while, if you don't have other plans for him?'

'Indeed, sir, I'm quite sure he will.'

Theophilus waited, but there was nothing further. He contemplated the urbane style of his son's reaction and felt a quiet pride.

'Then off you go, gentlemen. I've enjoyed your company.'

'And we yours, sir. Come on, Willie!'

And with that, off they went.

★

Elsewhere in the Tew residence, in a small conservatory overlooking the private dell to the rear of the house, Miss Tew, aged sixteen, had been quizzing her brothers' commanding officer.

'Captain Duvivier, tell me, sir, if you will, what is the most remote part of the world you have experienced?'

'Remote in the sense of distant and faraway, Miss Tew? Or remote in a figurative sense?'

'Both, I think, sir. But let us take them in their turn, if you please.'

'Certainly, Miss Tew.' Duvivier, with a smiling glance, anticipated the admonition of Miss Beaufoy seated nearby and shook his head almost imperceptibly, feeling the steady gaze of the questioner upon him.

'Because remoteness, I would say, has mainly to do with the sense of otherness one experiences from places. So, Miss Tew, the remotest place I know in that sense would be the Empty Quarter of the Arabian Desert, the Rub'h al Khali, where there is quite literally nothing but rocks and sand. How one might navigate a course across it is a matter of considerable interest—'

'And why should one wish to do that?'

'To map it, Miss Tew. To bring it, as it were, under control by quantifying distances which can only be judged approximately without modern measuring devices, to... lay yet another piece of the jigsaw of the world's surface, to eliminate the blank bits—'

'And are there many such unmapped regions, sir?'

'Quite a few still, Miss Tew. Enough to keep the cartographers busy for a while yet.'

'And you, captain? Shall you travel again to more remote places?'

'I sincerely hope so, Miss Tew. If the army will allow it. For travel is the greatest adventure by far; believe me, it is.'

'More so than battle, sir? My brothers would claim, I think, that battle must be the ultimate a man can experience?'

'But, Miss Tew, with respect, how could they know? Battle, believe me, is so appalling a thing that I shall speak no more of it to you. Travel is a marvellous thing; adventure and risk come in to it, of course, but they are hardly a *raison d'être* for it. No, travel celebrates the many and varied facets of God's jewel, the earth. We cut a diamond, do we not, Miss Tew, to enhance its natural beauty with an elegance that is human? So the two things combine, the human and the natural, and the result is something exquisite. Similarly, we celebrate the marvellous familiarity of the unfamiliar by getting close to it in the mundane ways travel requires, such as walking up mountains, finding drinkable water or a safe place to sleep the night through.'

'Captain Duvivier, I find your conversation fascinating.'

'You flatter me, Miss Tew.'

'No sir, indeed I do not.'

Here Mary Beaufoy rose at last from the vantage point from which she had discreetly monitored the exchanges between her charge and the handsome, elegant officer with his dreadful memento of war. It was as if his face had been taken apart and put back together just somewhat out of line, she mused. And Mary Beaufoy, a philosopher by inclination as well as from the necessity of her circumstances, had noted with admiration from the first the stoic dignity of manner and bearing which, no doubt, he had been obliged to cultivate in coming to terms with what was irreversible. Nicholas Duvivier had made a fine impression generally in the Tew household from the moment he had appeared as the guest of his two comparatively wayward subalterns. Mary Beaufoy allowed herself a veiled smile at the thought of Fred and Willie, and it briefly crossed her mind to pray that they might never experience the kind of suffering he must have endured.

As she rose, Miss Beaufoy sensed the presence of Frederick behind her.

'I say, Miss Beaufoy, do you imagine we might extricate Duvivier? My father has some wine to offer him, and Eleanor has monopolised him quite long enough.'

'Quite so, Mr Tew. One moment, if you please.'

But Eleanor was already moving.

'I think, sir, I am to release you to my father, so I shall do so. But perhaps we might speak again of such matters?'

Duvivier smiled as he rose to his feet.

'Of the anthropophagi?'

'And of men whose heads grow beneath their shoulders too, sir, if you please.'

'I shall please, Miss Tew. Although I fear I have nothing quite so exotic to offer.'

He was conscious of the steady, enquiring gaze of bright blue eyes. The poise of the girl was extraordinary for one hardly out of the nursery. Then she turned to her governess and went quickly from the room, as Fred and Willie came forward to him.

Chapter Two

From Miss Clough's house in Cambridge, Eleanor wrote to her friend and confidante, Mary Beaufoy, now charged with the instruction of the younger Tew daughters.

...it does seem a very extraordinary thing that, despite the unequivocal recent success of Miss Woodhead in the Mathematical Tripos, the University authorities still choose to withhold proper accreditation from women. In the circumstances one can understand and sympathise with the fighting spirit – yes, I think so – of Miss Davies at her college out at Girton, although one is not unaware of the different point of view from hers held by our own Miss Clough and, of course, Mr Sidgwick. One cannot but admire the sense of purpose and unremitting determination displayed by so many of those who have worked for the cause of women's education over recent years; it would be churlish in the extreme not to wish to make one's own contribution somehow or other. However, where I am concerned the question of 'somehow or other' looms large indeed. I too am to read for the Mathematical Tripos next year; most likely my father will have informed you of his correspondence with Miss Clough and the authorities to that end. I am confident that I shall manage a performance which will be creditable but not distinguished, for, from my knowledge of the marvellous achievements of intellect of which some members of the University repeatedly prove themselves capable, I know that I shall never make an original contribution to the subject which has meant so much

to me for so long. That could be a sadness, if one allowed oneself to brood upon it, but we guard against such self-indulgent sentimentalities here, in the tradition that is in the process of evolving, and quite rightly so too. Only, Mary dear, one needs one's friends in whom to confide, with whom one may share these deeply felt things.

Talking of friends, you will recall my fellow collegian, Miss Rowlandson, who visited us briefly in Leamington last year and who still speaks with admiration of your mastery of Livy. Apparently, it is her intention to spend part of the summer on a walking tour of Bavaria, partly for the constitutional benefits afforded by such exercise, partly to view the building works initiated by that strange young King Ludwig, who is only five years older than I myself. I have to say that I find it an extraordinary notion to wish to construct a replica of a medieval knight's castle in which to spend the remaining years of the nineteenth century, especially in view of the political turmoil still obtaining in Germany in consequence of that dreadful war against France of only two years ago. However, Miss Rowlandson has invited me to accompany her and since I love Germany both north and south, and since I love mountains and lonely places, I shall trudge the Bavarian Alps with her and bivouac in chalets and other remote spots. Do you recall Captain Duvivier? I have never forgotten what he told me of the fascination of travel and his own reasons for loving it as he did. He was of course a man of religious faith and saw this earth as 'God's precious jewel' – you may recall his analogy of the cut diamond – in a manner quite incomprehensible to me (poor Mamma!). But this earth in itself and for itself will do for me. I shall keep a journal in Bavaria, writing at night after simple fare among homely folk. Then perhaps I shall turn it into something more substantial. Eleanor Tew on Bavaria shall become a household term!

Interesting, is it not, how thoughts connect often apparently at random but in fact with a logic not constrained by time? Clearly, the memory interacts with the present function of mind. For instance, it was whilst I was engaged with Herodotus the other day – do you recall 'I wanted to know, so I went to see'? – that I thought of Captain Duvivier for the first time in many a long day. I am not sure what I want to know, though. I am not sure, indeed, whether knowing features so largely in my scheme of things, which must sound decidedly odd coming from one in my situation when this is viewed historically. Or perhaps I should say rather that, of the many forms of knowing, the conventional, accepted ones are not of the most pressing concern to me; that what I long for most, whatever it may be, will, when it eventually makes itself manifest to me, be something other than academic achievement or the kind of specific contribution Miss Davies has made to the cause of women, or fame of whatever kind, or formal honours.

In the meantime, though, I must busy myself with Bavaria and, indeed, to prepare myself I have been reading such literature of travel on the region as I can find. In a place such as Cambridge, of course, one does not have to look very far to find anything that exists in the way of books: one is totally spoiled by a comprehensive availability of everything in print which is of any value. There does not appear to be a very great deal on Bavaria in English, though, so perhaps I may make the attempt to remedy that – we shall see. What has appealed most so far has been illustrations of various kinds of the mountains from a number of sources. And how grand, how marvellously awe-inspiringly substantial they look! I long to be there, to make my way above the treeline and feel the rock against my hands. The scale and dimension of such things experienced at first hand must be truly awesome: one senses the efforts of artists to convey it but the imitation never quite does justice to the reality. Shall one ever

look upon the Himalayas, one wonders? And how would
they strike one, the great mountains of the earth? Would they
be simply too huge to apprehend? Or would they prompt the
same delicious sense of one's own insignificance in the scheme
of things? For we are so self-centred, we humans, are we not?
I am convinced we should be much more humble, to be
honest and realistic. And this, I suppose, is the kind of
knowledge which I find precious above all others. Perhaps 'I
wanted to know so I went to see' does, after all, touch me
more nearly than I had understood.

Dear Mary, such news! Thanks to generous Mr Sidgwick, we are to build a college too! At Newnham village.
Perhaps it will be named Newnham College. It seems quite
likely. Rather a good sort of name, don't you agree?
Newnham College, Cambridge. Yes, most decidedly.

Kiss all my darlings for me. When I think of you all,
which I do every day, I long to be with you, eating bread and
jam in the nursery, or doing something similarly companionable. But those days are irrevocably gone now. Is
Jemima still as messy as ever? Do you remember this?

The Tale of Jammy Jemmy,
the Messy Moppet

There was a child, named Jemima T,
Who, unlike the likes of you and me,
Found that with jam she was quite unable
To keep it on the nursery table.
Her little hands flew here and there,
Left sticky patches on her chair
And on the tablecloth around
Her place. And blobs of yellow, red and blue
Would decorate the carpet's hue.
'It's not very nice, you know,' they said,

'To be so messy with jam and bread.'
Said Jem, 'I can't see what's to do
Jam's nice to plunge your hands into
And hurl about a bit, so there!'
They said, 'You've got it in your hair!
If you can't learn to be more clever,
You'll have to wear a bib forever!'

*I was so proud of that when I wrote it for her. I suppose I
still am.*

★

In the summer of 1873 the Misses Eleanor Tew and Anna
Rowlandson kept their rendezvous at the Belgravia home of
Miss Rowlandson, where Miss Tew was briefly reunited
with her military brothers through the kind offices of
Lieutenant George Rowlandson, boon companion and
partner in high jinks to the newly gazetted Captains
Frederick and William Tew.

A dinner of somewhat more ceremonious an order than
usual, given the fact of the young ladies' departure from
these shores, was laid on to welcome Miss Tew into the
Rowlandson home. The Tews and their lieutenant travelled
hell for leather up to town for it, and would no doubt be
travellin' hell for leather back down again in the early hours
after cigars and claret, in time for grilled bones and a chop
or two before the morning parade. Meanwhile Mr Rowlandson and his good lady presided genially over the
occasion at which Lieutenant George, with the tacit
connivance of his father, assumed in a certain style the role
of master of ceremonies.

Thus the Cambridge ladies spent their last evening in
England before entraining from Blackfriars Station next day
in a quiet, decorous household transformed for a brief

moment of kind conviviality by young voices somewhat louder than those to which it was accustomed and hearty, heartfelt, military laughter.

Eleanor, who adored her brothers with a kind of motherly indulgence, was touched by the warm-hearted forethought of Lieutenant Rowlandson and made her feelings quite clear.

'Oh, I say, Miss Tew! It was the least a fellow could do!'

She was reminded of Frederick and William and their hero-worship of Nicholas Duvivier, and noted somewhat wryly the passing of the years.

Turtle soup was consumed by way of a beginning. Eleanor sat by Mr Rowlandson, with George to her right. Opposite, the Tews had Miss Rowlandson between them, with Frederick, the senior twin, by their hostess.

'So, Miss Tew. The mountains then, eh?'

'Indeed, sir.'

Mr Rowlandson eyed the young woman and noted the steady gaze, the composed dignity. Decidedly, there was something of consequence to her, something – as with Anna – that was not to be discounted or ignored. He was not sure he was entirely comfortable with it, for it was something which did not feature at all in the counting houses of the City.

'And what, then, might draw a lady such as yourself to these lonely, benighted regions?'

'Lonely, sir, most decidedly. Benighted not at all. One is given to understand from all reports and accounts that the native peasantry is disposed of a simple dignity and grace in their mundane lives which might put many a genteel metropolitan to shame.'

'Indeed? But... Popish, are they not?'

'They are a different brand of Christian from our home-grown versions, certainly.'

Here Eleanor prepared to steer deftly away from a potentially explosive topic, recalling her own mother and discerning from the attentive interest of both senior Rowlandsons that something of moment might come to be at issue. 'But the loneliness, sir. Just consider! And the grandeur of awesome heights…'

Anna, likewise on the *qui vive*, came swiftly and tactically into the conversation with her own diversionary comment. 'Eleanor, my dear! How very Radcliffean! Such a stylish mode of utterance—'

'Oh, nonsense, Anna. Anyone at all could turn a phrase as pedestrian—'

As it happened, they need neither of them have bothered.

'What can they be talkin' about? I say, Tews, your sister's just like mine! Fright'nin', I call it!'

The idea of George Rowlandson being frightened by anything at all was so palpably absurd that everyone laughed.

'Just attend to Miss Tew, George, dear.'

'Sorry, Mamma. Sorry, Miss Tew.'

'What I was intending to convey, sir, was that that very loneliness is what may draw one, by virtue of the contrast it represents to the normal, preoccupied lives we lead, whether here in the metropolis, in Cambridge or indeed in busy military circles. The illustrators are all taken with just that: it is evident in their drawings of gigantic rocks, huge forests inhabited only by wild, non-human life—'

'You takin' any weapons, El?'

'Sir! If you please! My mother—'

'Oh, sorry, Mrs Rowlandson.'

'I shall have my alpenstock, Fred.'

'Your what, Miss Tew?'

'My alpenstock, lieutenant. A stout walking stick with a spiked ferrule, sir. For fighting off wild boar.' Here Eleanor resisted the very strong temptation she felt at that moment to say 'fightin' orf'.

'Eleanor!'

'Intrepid I call it. That's the word – intrepid.'

Eleanor had noted her younger brother's admiration for her friend and was suddenly moved almost to tears by her own love for him and her affection for the kind friends among whom she dined that day. The Reverend Francis Lisle Bowles had got it pretty well right, she recalled, and she resolved to read the Dover Cliff s sonnet to Anna before they retired for the night. Which, in due course, she did.

At Dover Cliffs

On these white cliffs that, calm above the flood,
Uplift their shadowing heads, and, at their feet,
Scarce hear the surge that has for ages beat,
Sure many a lonely wanderer has stood,
And, whilst the lifted murmur met his ear,
And o'er the distant billows the still eve
Sail'd slow, has thought of all his heart must leave
Tomorrow – of the friends he lov'd most dear,
Of social scenes, from which he wept to part –
But if, like me, he knew how fruitless all
The thoughts that would full fain the past recall,
Soon would he quell the risings of his heart,
And brave the wild winds and unhearing tide,
The world his country and his God his guide.

Next day, at first light, they entrained for Munich, via the Channel packet.

From the 'Bavarian Journal' of Eleanor Tew

We had been advised to make for Partenkirchen and establish a base there as a point of departure for our planned excursions into the Oberland.

This we duly did, after several pleasant days' recuperation from our lengthy journey in palatial, elegant Munich, where we lodged in an unpretentious, homely inn, some distance from the fashionable centre of this impressive Bavarian metropolis. Delightful as this preliminary sojourn proved to be, however, metropolitan life was not what was in question where we were concerned and it was with some relief therefore, and a sense of getting back to the real purpose of our visit, that we proceeded, by diligence as recommended, to the little centre of Partenkirchen.

We had dined, on our second evening in Munich, with an academic acquaintance of Miss Clough, one Professor Doktor Jakob Steiner, a scholar pre-eminent in his field of ancient Roman history and, indeed, a former pupil at Berlin of the great pioneer of modern historical research, none other than Leopold von Ranke himself. Distinguished scholar that he was, Professor Steiner, together with his good lady, proved also to be an affable, considerate host, and during the course of the evening's conversation – conducted, we proudly record, very largely in the native language – it transpired that dear Miss Clough, ever assiduous in our interest, had forewarned the professor of our intentions and made enquiries on our behalf as to how we might best go about finding a forward base, so to speak, in the form of lodgings in or near Partenkirchen, whence we might sally forth into the wilds. And, indeed, an inn with which the professor was himself familiar from many a walking tour in the area had, it seemed, already been notified on our behalf and a room made ready for our use should we choose to avail ourselves of it! One would, of course, expect no less of any friend of Miss Clough, but how such small acts of kindness and consideration do smoothe one's way across the face of this earth! Since this is our first expedition of this kind, we are relieved and grateful to be assisted in this way.

One of these days, though, I am resolved to make my way, with or without my dear Anna, into remoter wildernesses, to find my own drinking water and secure my own safe place for the night. These phrases have a familiar echo as I write them. Someone has spoken to me in much this vein at some time, I am convinced of it, although oddly enough I do not recall who. I shall turn my mind to other thoughts and then, duly, I shall remember.

Having established ourselves, then, at the Gasthaus zum goldenen Hirsch, we resolved to acclimatise ourselves by following some of the easier trails through the forests around the various lakes in the immediate neighbourhood. The mountains, of course, are very close now, and it would be hard to do justice to them without resort to the kind of gothic mode of discourse by which Anna and I were able to deflect the conversation from the vexed topic of religion at dinner last week in Belgravia. But yes, the mountains. Massive, gargantuan outcrops of elemental rock topped at their craggy heights with snow and, above the treeline, truly dramatic spurs of rock, grey, fissured granite, and, no doubt, various other elements it would need a geologist to describe in specific terms. One is constantly aware of them for they impose their distinctive character upon the locality, their heights redolent of unlimited possibility. One is aware, for instance, that beyond them lie the Tyrol and Italy and a south fragrant with orange and lemon, where the sun invariably shines bright and warm on spectacular landscapes and domestic and public buildings of gorgeous historicity. One is aware, also, of the possibility of adventurous exploration of their own more altitudinal regions, and, indeed, I look forward with eager anticipation to the moment at which I shall emerge from the treeline onto the bare rock itself. That will be a moment to be savoured in the experience of it and cherished in the memory afterwards.

In the meantime, in preparation, we trudge our way manfully by dazzling lake and through fragrant forest, breathing in an air of these highland regions which already, within a matter of mere days, has had its beneficent effect upon our health and being, such that we both feel positively electric with energy and calmly confident in mind and spirit. Oh, wonderful Bavaria!

From Eleanor Tew to the Misses Tew in Leamington Spa

Such doings, darlings, just imagine! We have met, nay, almost stumbled upon the King of Bavaria!

This is how it was. We had made our way, Miss Rowlandson and I, effectively parallel with the border between Bavaria and Austria in the direction of Hohenschwangau, our purpose being to turn into the forest at Plansee or thereabouts in the direction of Linderhof, where this enigmatic young monarch is in the process of building a palatial hunting lodge. So we strode the trail through mighty forests of pine, larch and fir and then, pausing briefly for my dear Anna to adjust the lacing of her boot, we became aware of a third human presence nearby. Now, as seasoned travellers of some three weeks' adventurous experience, we have become aware of the necessity for absolute decorum vis à vis strangers. Not that we have encountered anything remotely akin to threat or menace of whatever kind, but quite simply in the interest of that ladylike demeanour so insisted upon by Miss Clough and Miss Davies in Cambridge; one is, as it were, that much more sure of one's ground at a decorous distance. However, it was immediately apparent that the young man, for such he was, was no peasant or vagabond denizen of the wilds but a very fine gentleman indeed. He was dressed in elegant tweed, almost certainly Scottish, with the Bavarian feathered hat and something akin to an ulster thrown around his shoulders. He was dark-haired, melancholic, handsome in a brooding, almost Byronic style, and he greeted us, in proper German of course, with grave composure, enquiring after our purpose with a courteous interest.

'Good afternoon, ladies.'

'Good afternoon, sir.'

Miss Rowlandson was first to respond, and we needed no exchange of glances to know immediately who this must be. Indeed, he could have been no other. Inwardly though, I applauded my friend's discretion in choosing the non-committal form of address. A king should be 'sire', of course, but there was nothing to show that this was anything other than a gentleman, and gentlemen speak on terms of equality with anyone. The ceremony of courtly modes of address would have been misplaced here.

'And whither are you bound, ladies, may I ask?'

'To view the building of the Linderhof lodge, sir. To ascertain whether the actuality is as lovely as the name implies it ought to be.'

'Most elegantly put, madam. You are English, are you not?'

'Indeed, sir. Can it be so obvious?'

'On the contrary. It is virtually not apparent at all.' This was spoken with the most pleasant and understanding of smiles. 'So, kinsfolk then. Or nearly.'

Here one recalled the German connection with our own royal family and acknowledged the point with a slight bow, although there is, as far as I am aware, no direct Wittelsbach link, if indeed any at all. But the gesture was a gracious one.

'You do us honour to acknowledge it, sir. And may we proceed, would you say, without hindrance, to view his majesty's building?'

'You may be sure of it, ladies. I bid you good day and a pleasant afternoon's viewing.'

'We thank you, sir.'

Miss Rowlandson and I responded to his dismissal with a slight inclination of the head, then he was gone, back into the *forest as silently and unexpectedly as he had appeared from it. Afterwards, as we strode onwards, Miss Rowlandson and I had the most entertaining exchange, thus:*

'It was he, was it not?'

'Undoubtedly it was!'

'And did he know?'

'Know?'

'Know we knew.'

'My dear, I feared you might give us away.'

'And you were right to do so, Eleanor. I allow it. But, there is a certain… aura, is there not?'

'The divinity that doth hedge a king? I noticed that he *dismissed us.'*

'I am inclined to the view that he did know that we knew.'

'I too.'

'And did it please him, do you imagine, to be treated as a mere gentleman?'

'My dear Anna, gentlemen are never 'mere', not even from the vantage point of a king.'

'True. I am properly admonished.'

'I think, indeed I observed that he was pleased, yes.'

'My own thought exactly.'

And that, my darlings, is how Misses Anna Rowlandson and Eleanor Tew, ladies of England, quite inadvertently came to make the acquaintance of His Wittelsbach Majesty, King Ludwig of Bavaria, the second of that name.

Kisses to Gwen, kisses to Rachel, kisses to Jemmy…

From the 'Bavarian Journal'

One night, not long after the experience recounted to my beloved sisters in Leamington Spa, we were witnesses to the sight and sound of an alpine thunderstorm.

Cosily ensconced in the quarters we shared at the *gasthaus*, reading, writing letters and journals after a nourishing meal consumed in the smoke-filled ordinary amongst sociable, local customers, our first apprehension of anything untoward was an unanticipated darkening of the sky, accompanied by distant rumblings.

'My dear,' says Anna, 'how very dark it has gone. And so suddenly. Perhaps we might turn up the lamps a little?'

'Indeed, let us do so. I think, you know, that we may be about to experience a mountain thunderstorm such, probably, as I recall in Verona once; at a place named, appropriately enough, Buffavento.'

'And how was it, your storm?'

'Very wet indeed. I shall record my impressions of this one exactly as it occurs.'

'You really are an incorrigible writer, Eleanor, although why writers should require correction I am not at all sure. Nevertheless, it is what we say, is it not?'

'Conventionally, it is so. True.'

As I uttered these words, there came from outside an enormous detonation, accompanied by an intense flash of blue which illuminated the snow-clad crags visible above and beyond the forests. We both started.

'That was involuntary.'

'Quite.'

'One could be apprehensive. Such a volume of noise.'

'One will not allow oneself to be.'

'Absolutely not.'

'I shall watch it from over by the window, and record my impressions instantly.'

'I shall continue to peruse my philosophic gentleman.'

'But first, my dearest Anna, do come and look at the rain. Such rain, indeed!'

Laterally, across the façade of the dark forest, there drove rippling sheets of silver-white water. There was a further deafening crash of thunder, agony to the hearing, and blue light of an intense, electric hue leaped along a range of livid, rocky peaks.

Sitting with my notebook by the window, which opened onto our tiny balcony with its carved, wooden rail, I, Eleanor Tew, found myself considering for the first time ever the possibility of fear. And yet, I noted, outside and below, the inhabitants of Partenkirchen went imperturbably on with things. I espied an *Einspanner*, an open vehicle, trundling off into the blinding downpour, its occupants swathed in waterproof covers against the wet. I thought, too, of my military brothers. In the action of battle men must learn to face without flinching an enemy whose intention it is to mete out death. To do that they must first face themselves too. Had Fred and Willie faced themselves, I wondered?

Certainly they would never have put it in those terms, but surely they must have done, one way or another. And then it was that I understood with delight how the adventure of travel and the novelty of the experiences it affords can stimulate the intellect to sharp acts of observation. And with this realisation there came to me a moment of deep contentment, an apprehension of joy such as I had rarely known, if indeed I ever previously had at all. In the lamplight, to my rear, my dear Anna read on imperturbably oblivious to all but the blandishments of her philosophic gentleman. In that moment, however, I believe that I found – quite possibly without yet having fully realised it – a purpose to fulfil me. I shall travel the lonely places of this world and record, in writing, my experience of them. The vantage point of the lady traveller, although not entirely without precedent, will be sufficiently novel for our time; it will also furnish, by dint of its capacity for implication, the opportunity for sharp, dissenting commentary upon the ways of our own world.

Outside there was silence. The rain had stopped. The storm had gone on its way down the Alpine ranges.

★

And now, the Oberland. The high places. The words have a dramatic enough ring to them, although the reality, first apprehended at some distance, seems quite simply to beggar description. On further reflection, though, it does occur to me that such a thought must seem singularly defeatist for one with even minimal pretensions of a literary order. One may only hope that the discerning reader will recognise an acknowledgement of difficulty rather than an admission of failure.

In this connection I recall that, when I spoke recently of the grandeur of awesome heights at the Rowlandson home, my dear friend found cause there to draw attention to the gothic tenor of my phrase by a reference to the language of Mrs Radcliffe, and, indeed, one is led to wonder whether that particular mode may not in fact be the most appropriate to render the essential character of the experience of altitudinal terrains, although... But I shall withhold my qualification for the moment, for reasons that will duly become apparent.

To continue in the literary vein for a brief moment, it is worth recording, it seems to me – and oh, what may lurk behind that ostensibly most diffident of Cambridge locutions! – that the Augustan practice of finding an appropriate model amongst the ancients for a style most conducive to the effective rendering of a particular theme was indeed not without point. I am determined, however, that I shall not resort to Mrs Radcliffe before I have explored the resources of Eleanor Tew. The search for a style, for an appropriate register – in the musical sense – of utterance shall be an act of self-examination and discovery.

However, I wrote earlier of my anticipation of that exquisite moment when, after the steep and arduous trek across uplands and through forest, one would at last find oneself in direct contact with the mountain itself.

It would be easy to romanticise experience of this kind. After all, we name mountains, and in doing so we invest them with an identity which distorts our perception of them even as it familiarises and renders them less fearsome, which is not such a good idea, as I see it...

But first, my narrative. It has long been the practice here to graze cattle on the uplands for periods of several months at a time, and the creatures are accompanied to the higher reaches by a hardy young woman who remains with them for the duration of their sojourn; her alpine dwelling – since an alp, despite conventional usage, is technically an upland pasture – is a crude chalet or *Sennhut* in which she abides, alone, for many a long month. Evidently, the sterling character of these young *herd girls*, their fortitude and ability to endure the solitude of their exile, cannot but find its acknowledgement among those who benefit by it – for these young women make an essential contribution to the economy of their villages by their care of the cattle which represent the wealth of the community. Hence, their return from the highlands is celebrated by the village in a public act of gratitude, regard and affection.

The *herd girl*, then, is one type of distinctive local figure who epitomises the strength and moral character, the simple dignity and human consequence of the local peasantry here. There is of course a variety of others, of whom but one shall concern us for the moment. I shall refer to him as the mountain guide, for without him the matter of survival in these high places of the earth would be problematic indeed.

So, when at last we decided, my dear Anna and I, that we were ready for an excursion into the Oberland, we set about the matter by consulting our kind and considerate hosts, Herr Dedler and his wife. For our acquaintance with Professor Steiner of Munich had, it was clear, caused us to be singled out from the time of our arrival for a certain favour, which took the discreet form of an avuncular, indulgent concern. Our host, with his generous build and rollicking mustachios, was never too preoccupied to discuss the merits of a particular item on a menu lovingly and expertly composed by his good wife in conjunction with Johan, the cook. For they were accustomed to country appetites, these kindly folk, and were concerned for our well-being, given what must have seemed to them the minute portions of food which were sufficient for our needs.

So one evening we duly broached the subject of the highlands, to the anxious concern of Frau Dedler, summoned instantly by her husband.

'One thing we must insist upon, young ladies, is that if you do go you are accompanied by a guide who knows the mountains. You shall approach this in the proper manner or not at all.'

We were grateful for his solicitude. The proposition of the mountains had begun indeed to loom as somewhat formidable. But they were what we had come for; they were all around us, magnificent, menacing, more than a little intimidating in what they invited us to. But we were resolved.

'Ludwig Rendl, I think.'

'My dear, the very man.'

And thus it was that we came to make the acquaintance of our guide to the Bavarian Oberland.

Ludwig Rendl was a man of middling age, lean and vigorous and weather-beaten, a man of forest and mountain whose sense of earth, rock and sky struck us, when we came to comprehend it, as little short of uncanny. Our experience of Herr Rendl came, once again, to lodge in the memory as one of the mind-expanding, truly enriching aspects of travel to which I have previously referred in a somewhat different context. Ludwig Rendl is not to be met with in the fashionable streets of London or of any metropolis. However...

Negotiations were entered into, terms of payment agreed, acquaintance established, a plan of action discussed. We were to make a series of preliminary excursions, it transpired, through the deep forest and out on to the higher upland before we attempted anything like an approach to the rock itself. But the matter-of-fact manner in which the notion of 'an approach to the rock' was raised was in itself enough to send a thrill of apprehensive anticipation through me, and I knew without needing to verify the point that my dear friend was feeling exactly as I was. Here we were, at last at what we had come for, and close enough now to that actuality, intimidating as it might seem, which was the *raison d'être* for our journey thither. With no more than a few measured words, Herr Rendl had brought us squarely face to face with the concrete character of what had been, up to that moment, we realised, no more than a theoretic intention. For here was a man of a very different order of existence from our own, but one, I understood, who was as comfortably at ease with the familiarity of his milieu as we were with ours. The insight was in some way inexpressibly thrilling to me, for the way in which it seemed to confirm and corroborate vague intimations of similar perceptions which had been, one way or another, peculiar to my own particular and idiosyncratic mode of rumination for as long as I could remember. However... Herr Rendl, it was clear from his appraising glances, would be insisting upon a degree of stamina and strength in us which was to be actively determined.

And so it proved to be. Our first outing took us into thick forest between Linderhof and the Plansee, but the route was a very different one from the accredited trail we had wandered on the occasion when we happened upon a certain fine and kingly gentleman.

But the deep forest must needs be described, and in the first instance I must allow that my phrase 'deep forest' is but a poor equivalence for that most evocative of German coinages, the 'Urwald', with its resonances of primeval antiquity.

From the trail, then, one plunges into a dense world of forest where the canopy of foliage effectively blots out the sky. One thus finds oneself in a region of intense gloom, silent and still to initial perceptions, although subsequently, as one adjusts to these surroundings, less and less so. For the forest, with its row after apparently orderly row of straight, bare, brown trunks – of giant pines, of green, mossy velvet oak and larch, its shining white columns of colossal plane trees – is alive, breathing it seems almost, cognisant of living presences. There is about it a timeless-ness intimidating to contemplate, for the apprehension of this brings with it an overwhelming sense of the mo-mentary character of a human lifespan. What is true of age measurable only in aeons of time, as with the rock of the high mountains, is equally so of the Urwald.

We make our way into this other world as our guide bids us, trudging at a steady pace as he determines. And several things become apparent. In the first instance, we realise with a shock of recognition that he knows exactly where he is, as he presumably identifies a predetermined route by reference to individual and particular features of the scene, though what exactly we fail to ascertain.

Then again, the floor of the forest is not level, rather rough and uneven, with rapid ascents and descents which render it at once more interesting, if less comfortable of negotiation. We understand then, too, that the pace at which we are proceeding, as determined by Ludwig Rendl, is a carefully calculated one, that he is making his estimate of our capabilities, observing our reactions to what is as strange and novel to us as it is familiar to him. One is filled with confidence in this extraordinary man, and with awe at what is implied in his proceeding of a positively encyclo-paedic knowledge of the natural life of the region and the capacities of human beings to cope with it. And yet this is a 'simple' man, conventionally a Bavarian peasant. I am at once filled with a deep sense of humiliation, aversion to and shame at the shallow nature of the genteel perception of this, our marvellous world and its varieties; I understand more clearly than ever before the grounds for my dear father's passion for the sciences of the natural world and I am confirmed even more strongly in my sense of a travel-ler's vocation. For, oh, the prodigious intelligence of even the humblest of our human kind!

That evening, on our return to the inn at Partenkirchen, we said little of the day, Anna and I, but our silence was companionable as never before and rich with a quiet joy.

★

We must have passed our examination and assessment, in its way every bit as stringent as a Tripos, for it was made known to us some while later, after a further series of excursions through forest and upland, that Ludwig Rendl was proposing a sally onto the rock for the forthcoming week, all things being equal.

'But he must watch the weather,' said our host, with Frau Dedler nodding seriously by his side. 'This is of great importance. But Ludwig will know – and some good time in advance – when conditions will be as they should be.'

'Do you mean to say,' asks Anna, 'that he can predict weather conditions?'

'Most certainly, young lady. In the mountains one acquires this knowledge from birth, for it is essential to survival. One simply could not live a functional life without it.'

Ein tätiges Leben. A life for doing things in. Yes, yes!

★

It would be, indeed it is easy to take the romantic view of the high mountains: they invite hyperbole by their massive splendour, the sheer scale of their dimensions in space and time, against which we human creatures are as mere momentary ants. I am determined, however, to resist this eminently understandable temptation in the interests of what shall be, one hopes, a more efficacious treatment of the subject. Efficacious by virtue of its greater realism, that is.

In the first instance, then, one traverses the open emptiness of the high pastures, littered with crazy jumblings of stark, often gigantic rockery. One is frequently led to wonder how these massy outcrops came to be where they are. Did they crash down, lightning-struck, from the heights above, in thunderous trajectory, to bury themselves thus in the softness of the lower terrain? One is aware, as one progresses higher, that these are regions not subject to the mean constraints of mechanical, human time. Here, other imperatives apply; unimaginable vistas of inexorable, evolutionary time suggest themselves...

Even here, though, there are traces of human culture – the occasional *Sennhut* nestling beneath colossal rock clusters, the distant tinkle on the wind of the inevitable alpine cowbells. What is most striking, most disturbing to acknowledge, though at the same time almost, as it were, thrilling to experience is what I can only describe as the recognisable familiarity of it all, of the sense of non-human time which obtains in the high expanses. I say non-human, but at the same time one is at one with the scene, one belongs there, one recognises one's own tiny place in this unimaginably vast scheme of things...

We come, at long last, to the rock, at first a gentle gradient, boulder-strewn, littered with the stony rubble of ages. Ludwig Rendl offers technical advice on how to negotiate the screes ahead, as, now corded together, we pick our way at his steady pace to where the beginnings of a ridge incline rather more sharply upwards. And high above us there looms a mighty peak, glittering gnarled grey-white below its cap of snow, radiant, dazzling as the mid-morning sun now catches and illumines it. Once again I am filled with an inexpressible elation. For some reason my name comes back to me. Literally, for my mind had emptied itself of such extraneous impedimenta, in order, no doubt, the better to apprehend the prodigious scenes before us. Now, though, as from faraway I hear the sounds voiced thus: Eleanor Tew! I am Eleanor Tew! I could raise the most tremendous shout of triumph here, but alas! Even here I am still, whatever else I may be, an English lady, so I do not do so.

There was, it transpired, no question of an ascent to the peak itself, even if we had entertained any such or similar notion. Ludwig Rendl led us expertly on to the rock as far as he reasonably could, then, as we rested to take a morsel of sustenance, explained something of the climbing techniques necessarily involved in such an ascent. And, having been thus put to the test both in the forest and on the mountain, and having now listened – as dispassionately as he had taught us to – to his tactfully worded assessment of skills and physical capacities as well as his estimates of risk, we were brought to appreciate the impossibility of what we just might have thought we were about, although, discussing the matter with dear Anna back down amid the cosy homeliness of our inn quarters, we were both brought to the realisation that what we had imagined to be in store for us had in actuality been nothing more than the haziest of suppositions. Chastening, of course, in the first instance, but, in the light of what we now knew of the mountains, from having experienced them at first hand through the wise guidance of one who was also a philosopher and acquaintance worthy of the highest esteem, any idea we might have vaguely entertained of a girlish scramble up some rocks was appropriately reduced to what it was worth. In the privacy of our quarters at the goldenen Hirsch we did in fact allow ourselves the indulgence of a wild bout of nursery laughter, such as I often used to delight in with the Tew moppets and our dear nurse in Leamington Spa, at the thought.

Prior to this, we had parted from Ludwig Rendl with expressions of regard and esteem. For he had cared for us and instructed us, led us to an enlarged sense of life's possibilities, no less, with something akin to the love of a father for his children. And, indeed, I am resolved that my own dear father shall know of this, because he of all people will understand and appreciate the close affinity I perceive between himself, an English gentleman of science, and this Bavarian mountain ranger. I understand that Mr Rowlandson, alas, could never be so disposed, so I shall refrain from further comment on the matter. We shall write, too, to Professor Steiner, for we are greatly in his debt. Also to dear Miss Clough in Cambridge.

Meanwhile we prepare for our imminent departure from these alpine regions, and Anna searches her portfolio of sketches, drawings and watercolours of mountain and forest, a truly prodigious compilation, for something we may leave with the Dedlers, to be conveyed as a mark of our appreciation to Ludwig Rendl, whom we are unlikely to meet again.

From the 'Journal and Commonplace Book' of Eleanor Tew, 1874

Transitions, I find, can and should be stimulating, and one is singularly fortunate to be in a position to travel – from England to Germany, from England to Italy, from Leamington Spa to Cambridge, from Cambridge to London and so on. This is of course a fact of rare human experience, acknowledged and celebrated by a variety of literary figures, including a fair number of ladies of more than usually adventurous disposition. And it is a matter of pride to me personally that it is so.

Here in Cambridge now, as I write this, autumn turns to winter, which closes in upon us, enveloping all – trees, Backs, Fens, college buildings – in its icy gloom. Mists swirl about venerable archways dimly illumined; we wrap up against the cold, look to food, drink and fire for comfort. The pattern of this must be primordial, it would seem, and, even as the thought occurs, I begin to discern something which it seems to me is of no little significance, something which perhaps ought to be much more readily acknowledged than it is, that is, the continuity which extends from primitive modes of existence even up to the most refined levels of what we are pleased to call civilisation. For this age in which I live and write down these thoughts asserts too absolute a divide between what we are now and what was before. It is a false and foolish view of things and one which does us no credit. I shall therefore contest it, using the experience of travel to do so.

How frequently these days do I think back to the summer of last year in Bavaria. I know too that my dear Anna does the same, for on the occasions when we meet, these busy days, we invariably find reference, implied or otherwise, in our conversation to events and personalities of that time. For the experience of mountain and forest, of novel and invaluable acquaintance – Professor Steiner, the Dedlers, Ludwig Rendl – was truly an improving, edifying thing. We are the richer, Anna and I, for having lived that time as we did, and one cannot but be grateful to circumstance – if indeed that is possible, though I rather suspect it is not, since one cannot express gratitude to impersonal and random forces – for having endowed us with the privileges of wealth and the disposition to take us there.

Transitions, yes. The experience of Bavaria enhances and enriches the continuing experience of Cambridge, of being who one is.

The mathematics proceeds apace; it is demanding, taxing work, often imbued with the most intense intellectual excitement. Its abstractions represent a cool and necessary counterbalance to my more worldly preoccupations, but much as I enjoy it and find stimulation in it, and however creditably I am determined to perform in the Tripos, I know that my early instinct and apprehensions were true and exact. I could never excel in this field, not to the degree one would wish. But where once this might have proved a sadness, I now know that the world beyond such considerations, what waits out there with Bavaria so to speak, is of infinitely greater importance to me.

Chapter Three

By the time she had completed her undergraduate studies at the new college of Clough Hall in Cambridge, Eleanor Tew was also well on the way to completing a final draft of the manuscript of her *Bavarian Journal*, which, with accompanying illustrations from the portfolio of Miss Rowlandson, was destined to take its place in the 'Books for Travellers' series put out by a well-known Piccadilly publishing house, in crown octavo cloth bound, at six shillings per copy.

During the summer months following her departure from the university in 1875, Eleanor sojourned with French relatives in Normandy, where she put the final touches to her manuscript and reflected upon her future, exchanging copious correspondence with her father in Leamington Spa.

She had, as she herself had predicted, acquitted herself with credit in the Mathematical Tripos, taking a sound second. She had long since decided, however, that the world of academe was not where her future lay, given the increasingly imperative fascination to which she found herself subject with a notion of wilderness and human life lived at a level of simple necessity which would contrast absolutely – she surmised – with the rococo sophistications of the world into which she had been born. To venture out into the larger world, into such a milieu, to find her own place within it would represent daring enterprise at its quintessential. It was a dream which would find its particular and local form in due course, she knew.

Throughout the summer months of 1875, Eleanor walked the woods and grounds of the modest but proud Normandy château near Bayeux, which had belonged to the French line of her father's family for the best part of a thousand years, and pondered the matter of a course of action.

She had of course fathomed the reasons for her mother's ready acquiescence in the scheme of a Normandy sojourn broached by herself and her father. There were eligible French cousins abounding, an extensive family acquaintance reaching far into the best of French society.

Theophilus, too, from the depths of his den in Clarendon Crescent, had wryly, ironically, agreed to the scheme. For he knew his daughter too well to imagine that she would prove susceptible to the butterfly blandishments of urbane but lightweight young French noblemen, and in this he understood Eleanor far better than his good lady her mother, who chose to ignore that aspect of her daughter, if indeed she did not merely fail to register it at all. For Charlotte Tew, now ageing, hypochondriac, paralysingly devout, had never been at ease with her eldest daughter and had, dutifully and with relief, been only too glad to leave her to Theophilus and the good Doctor Barnes. Where that had led her was now rather the matter in question. Perhaps something would come of the French interlude. One could only hope. Meanwhile, the matter of Rachel's marriage had begun to loom and it seemed not unlikely that Gwendolen would follow soon after. With her religion, her constitution, her marriageable daughters, Charlotte Tew had much to amuse and preoccupy her.

Theophilus took a somewhat different view of things. In the first instance, everything he had plotted and planned with Barnes for Eleanor, over dozens of glasses of claret companionably consumed in the den, had been realised. Now it was a question of the way forward for her, the principle of her independence having been tacitly established despite Charlotte's occasional ritual protestations. For there was sadly little enough sympathy between Theophilus Tew and his lady wife. Somewhat over thirty years previously he had married an enchanting young woman who had borne him six healthy children and managed his household, through the servants, with consummate capability. But where the deeper things of life were concerned... At least he had Eleanor, and Barnes, and claret and the consolations of philosophy. The continual exchange of correspondence with his eldest daughter and his own and Barnes's discussion of her thoughts and observations were thus the focus of his emotional existence now.

'It keeps on coming back, does it not, my dear Tew, to this fascination with the lonely places of the earth?'

'It does, Barnes, yes. And it is all there in the *Bavarian Journal*, as you shall shortly see.'

'Is it not, if I may say so, a somewhat slender foundation on which to build life's edifice?'

'The thought had occurred to me too, my dear friend, I will not deny it. But on reflection, you know, Barnes, it is a point of departure from which expansion and development may well ensue.'

'True.'

'However, it is, I have to say, an unfocussed, unspecific thing. This is what concerns me, I allow.'

'Then perhaps we might take steps to focus it, my dear Tew. I mean, what do you imagine Miss would say, perhaps, to the idea of a period of reading and study in the archives of the Royal Geographical Society?'

'Barnes, you are a genius! What a capital notion!'

'I am glad you are agreeable, Tew. So perhaps we might broach it?'

'With caution, my dear doctor, with caution. We shall…
propose it. We may even urge it a little, don't you think?'

'I do, Tew. I do.'

★

That year Eleanor saw out the rest of the summer amongst
her French cousins, returning briefly to her home in
Leamington Spa before proceeding to London, to take up
residence there awhile and avail herself of the resources of
the Royal Geographical Society.

In Leamington there were lengthy discussions between
her father and herself, with Doctor Barnes present on
occasion to add his contribution. The *Bavarian Journal* was
published, too, that autumn, to the delight of the other Tew
daughters, the amazement of the military twins and the
quiet satisfaction of Theophilus and Barnes.

The notion of something rather in the style of a traditional grand tour was broached and aired before being
tactfully discounted.

'… for you may imagine, sir, that dancing with Russian
princes in Vienna is not exactly what I have in mind.'

'I think we appreciate that, do we not, my dear Barnes?'

'Most certainly we do, Tew. The notion of a tour, my
dear young lady, was, I suppose, mooted in the interest of a
certain procrastination – not that there is any urgency in
these things. But we thought it might afford an opportunity
to take stock, to explore such possibilities as might suggest
themselves. For the stimulus of travel is, as we all know,
not to be underestimated.'

'That is most true, doctor. It is precisely the reason I am
inclined the way I am. But the experience must be something more than social, sir. For me it must be in some
way… prodigious. If, that is, I am to find in it such metaphor as I hope may enable me to make constructive and

useful comment upon certain features of our accepted ways and beliefs. And besides, gentlemen, it should be amusing, should it not? "What larks!" as Mr Dickens has it, somewhere. I am drawn to the notion of high spirits and adventure – and indeed, is it not significant, Father, doctor, that I may express myself thus only in your company and no one else's? Ladies simply may not hoot with laughter; we all know this, but I am often brought to wonder whether gentlemen, even intelligent ones, can appreciate what is involved in the way of constraint that such a prohibition imposes? Can you imagine, for instance, how much at times I have envied my brothers, with their free and easy military manners? Or what is implied in Miss Austen, expressionless, making the most outrageously funny comments on what she never fails to observe of the absurdities of our human condition? No, gentlemen. The social honing that would be the only end of the grand tour for a lady as such – and what other could there possibly be, conventionally speaking? – does not commend itself. What I require is a true and wholly individual independence; something, I fear, which is not easily come by in our particular reaches, or indeed in any reaches of European society.'

Theophilus Tew and Samuel Barnes exchanged mutually congratulatory glances of satisfaction at this, marvelling at what their concern and forethought had contributed to the formation of Eleanor to bring her to this lucidity of mind, voiced with all the authentic ring of the best of Cambridge to it. But even as they did so, the two elderly gentlemen could not but acknowledge the disturbing justice of her words.

'Very well, then, my dear.' Theophilus drew the discussion to a conclusion. 'You shall go to your Uncle and Aunt Tew in Bloomsbury, and apply yourself to deliberation.'

'Thank you, Papa.'

They rose as she took her leave, the two gentlemen, and watched her go. Theophilus poured claret.

'Impressive, Tew. Almost a new breed of lady. Well, perhaps not quite that, but certainly a rare one, and something most decidedly beyond the ordinary.'

'True, Barnes, true. We may allow ourselves a certain pride, I think, in what has been achieved. But what will become of her, do you imagine? For I am sure that I cannot.'

★

In London, Eleanor Tew consulted maps and gazetteers and pondered the matter of mountain ranges. She was aware that the greatest travellers were those who travelled alone, in the belief that any fellow countryman would, as it were, come between them and the land over which they travelled. But how was this to be achieved? She knew that even her father, liberal in his views and sympathetic to her purposes, would not, indeed could not – by virtue of the social constraints upon him and probably also by virtue of his own affection for her, his most favoured daughter – allow quite so radical a departure from accepted practice as yet. The problem seemed insuperable at this stage in her life, so she resolved to put that aspect of things to one side for the moment, until she had determined upon a specific project and destination. As this time two possibilities presented themselves: one was the Picos de Europa, little known to the English traveller or indeed, as far as Eleanor was able to determine, to any of the peoples of Northern Europe. The other was the Pyrenees. An expedition from the Atlantic to the Mediterranean, or possibly, but less likely, the other way, would be an undertaking of worth and interest. Besides which, she had the advantage of excellent French, whereas the Spanish language would have to be studied from its beginnings and even then, when one had acquired a working, rudimentary knowledge of Castilian, there was no guarantee that this would prove the most efficacious mode of communication with the mountain folk, who presumably spoke a dialect, or dialects even. One could, of course, consult appropriate authorities in Cambridge or, even more nearly, in the metropolis itself. Her lawyer uncle Tew, with his extensive range of acquaintance and prodigious, proud, Dickensian familiarity with the life of the capital, would be glad to find her leads into appropriate circles... But no, she mused; the idea of so laborious a preparation for what was to be, after all, nothing more than another European excursion was, she thought, not for her at this stage. So the Pyrenees it should be, it seemed. There could be another book for travellers in it, after all, and one well worth writing. Given such a proposition, Messrs Chatto & Windus would hardly demur, after the undoubted success of the *Bavarian Journal*. 'From the Atlantic to the Mediterranean; a Pyrenean Excursion'.

From where she sat, Eleanor looked out across the Gore to the park where, as rain swept across a darkling autumn scene, lamps were being lit both inside and out, distant and near, to enliven the gloom of early evening. But a specific resolution gave purpose to one's endeavours, and her heart was lighter as she rode home through the twilight to her Uncle and Aunt Tew in Taviton Street.

From The Tatler & Bystander, *April 1876*

Miss Eleanor Tew, who, readers will recall, was one of an early generation of Miss Ann Jemima Clough's ladies at the now well-established Clough Hall in Cambridge, is to make a further excursion following the success of her *Bavarian Journal* in the well-known 'Books for Travellers' series. This time Miss Tew has the intention of walking the length of the Pyrenees from the Atlantic to the Mediterranean, and at the moment the question of how she is to accomplish this is under consideration. Readers will recall that Miss Tew was accompanied in her previous, Bavarian excursion by a Cambridge friend, Miss Anna Rowlandson, who was to furnish the popular *Bavarian Journal* with a variety of delightful illustrations of mountain, plant and forest life. This time, regrettably, it appears that Miss Rowlandson is not available to accompany her friend. 'The question of a travelling companion is, quite clearly, crucial,' Miss Tew told me. 'I am applying myself to the matter with as much diligence and consideration as will go into the actual planning of the expedition itself. Though perhaps "expedition" is overdoing it somewhat.'

When I queried this qualification, Miss Tew explained that, splendid as they undoubtedly were, the Pyrenees were still European and as such effectively 'on the doorstep'. It is her firm intention to strike out one of these days much further afield. There was Arabia, for instance. The Empty Quarter. True, it had recently been crossed by an Englishman, but nevertheless... The high, empty places of the world too; the thought of such terrains was tempting, was it not, the thought of these high, wild, lonely places with their sprinklings of indigenous peoples living lives very different from our own and yet no doubt preoccupied, as we are, with basic human concerns? Sustenance, warmth and comfort in the cold, pride in a child, admiration for marksmanship, for a wise judgement, for a story well told... Persia, Afghanistan, Tibet... For a brief moment I was vouchsafed the privilege of a glimpse into the imagination of this intrepid and fascinating lady, and wondered at such an appetite for adventure, with what it implied of so sanguine a disregard for discomfort, danger even, and not only these but, possibly most important of all, the capacity to withstand solitude for substantial lengths of time.

'That was something I learned from Bavarian *herd girls*,' averred this remarkable lady, 'who spend months at a time alone in the high pastures of the Oberland with only their beasts for company. They are possessed of a strength of character, a moral equilibrium, these humble country folk, which is not to be forgotten once encountered and indeed can only be marvelled at and acknowledged in humility.'

'You, an English lady and mathematical scholar of the University of Cambridge assert this of peasants?'

'I do,' said Miss Tew firmly. 'It is beyond any question of doubt.'

'Society might find this hard to accept, do you not think?'

'Then society must needs adjust its views.'

'And do you see it, then, as at least in part your purpose to convey such truths as you see them to a more conventional readership?'

'In part I suppose that is a purpose, yes. But in the first instance the end of my travels is something other.'

'And what may that be?'

'One might say 'self-indulgence'; I prefer "curiosity". "I wanted to know, so I went to see".'

'A quotation, Miss Tew?'

'From Herodotus, the Greek historian.'

'So, I hope we may look forward to further communication from you in the future, Miss Tew.'

'That will be my pleasure.'

From Eleanor Tew to Theophilus Tew, Esquire

Dear Father,

Concerning my intended Pyrenean enterprise, I have a proposition to put to you which, I trust, you will do me the favour of considering with due seriousness, given your usual practice in these matters.

The proposition is this: that I invite Mary Beaufoy to travel at my expense as my companion on the expedition. Such an arrangement would be, it seems to me, doubly advantageous in that, firstly, it would provide me with the companionship I seek to make the enterprise viable; in the second place, it would represent a generous acknowledgement on the part of the Tew family of the service rendered over the years by one whose teaching has been of inestimable value to myself (you will recall Uncle Hubert's acknowledgement of the excellence of that French which is the product of Mary's instruction) as well as my sisters.

I shall not of course be making any mention of this notion of mine to Mary herself before I have heard from you on the matter. I do trust, though, that the inconvenience of finding a temporary replacement for Mary as mentor to Jemima would not prove unduly onerous. May I hope therefore that this idea of mine meets with your approval and endorsement?

Your loving and dutiful daughter…

Chapter Four

With grave courtesy and a private resolve to use patience and such other palliative virtue as he could command, Theophilus Tew braved his wife's tea-table, where he found her in earnest conversation with a young clergyman in a cassock who was introduced as Father Brownlow. The name was not unfamiliar to Theophilus. Rupert Brownlow, author of the currently fashionable *Devotional Sonnets*, combined the haunted looks of an El Greco mystic with the urbane manners of the Oxford Movement. He was precisely the kind of clergyman – or priest, as Charlotte would no doubt have insisted he be called – to appeal to impressionable ladies of a certain age and disposition.

Theophilus seated himself, accepted tea and contemplated the scene; the imaginative and intellectual distance from his den, with Barnes and claret, to this sanctuary of his wife's was so enormous that he could rarely now find it in himself to make the journey of a few household yards from one to the other. There were, it is true, no crucifixes or other obvious religious icons in evidence, but here it seemed daylight was weaker and dialogue joined with the bated breath of sanctity, a self-indulgent religiosity which he found as abhorrent as it was aesthetically repulsive. For theirs had become an ugly age, he mused, as he cast a longingly reminiscent glance back to the more elegant, more rumbustious decades of his early manhood. And here was this young fellow – personable, of unimpeachable manners, a scholar of some kind of intelligence presumably – caught up in that movement from the '40s which had swept the Church of England, or much of it, into a manic fervour of the most credulous kind... Impatience and aversion stirred within him; he resolved to be firm with Charlotte.

'My dear,' he said at length when they sat alone together, 'I have come to you to talk over a proposition I have had from Eleanor which, since it will affect the household, should be your concern as well as mine.'

'Theophilus, what Miss Eleanor does these days is, as you are aware, of little moment where I am concerned. She, with your connivance, has chosen to follow a course which I cannot find it in me to approve as one appropriate to the situation of a lady. And one day you will have to answer for what—'

'My dear,' Theophilus interrupted brusquely despite his earlier resolve, 'the matter is a small one, but perhaps of more moment to one we value than it might occur to us in our ease to appreciate. I trust that your sentiments of charity extend to an approval of what might bring benefit and reward to one who has served us faithfully and to great effect over the years. I am referring, madam, to Miss Beaufoy. Eleanor has suggested Miss Beaufoy be invited to accompany her on the walking tour of the Pyrenean mountain range she is proposing to embark upon as a possible subject for her next book.'

'But... Jemima? Really, sir. How can you contemplate this? The idea is a preposterous one—'

'Charlotte, I have to say I am quite discountenanced by your words. It seemed to me that not only would this solve the problem of a companion but it would also constitute a fittingly generous reward as well as an acknowledgement of the regard and affection in which we hold Miss Beaufoy for the years she has devoted to us. For she has contrived to inculcate in our daughters a genuine love of antique culture as well as a technical proficiency in the French language which has been noted with approbation by my Norman cousins whenever our girls have had cause to display it. The matter of Jemima's continuing instruction is easily solved. It shall be, madam. I am resolved to authorise it, Miss Beaufoy being willing.'

'Miss Beaufoy is a paid employee, sir. The matter of her will hardly comes into question.'

'Nonsense, madam. She is a faithful retainer who shall be treated with the respect she deserves.'

There was more Theophilus could have said, a great deal more, having once again hoped against hope that he and his wife might find it in them to come an amicable agreement over Eleanor's proposal. But, seeing that it was not to be, Theophilus, with no more than a modicum of regret now, allowed his thoughts to turn briefly to another kind of house across the town, to which his bachelor friend, Barnes, had introduced him.

From the Journal of Eleanor Tew

One is unprepared, quite unprepared I now appreciate, for the splendour of the Pyrenees, and there are reasons of some interest why this should be so.

To begin with, this particular range of mountains, of all ranges thus close to home, if I may so express myself, is of enormous general historical interest.

From the maps it appears to form a natural barrier between France and Spain and physically it does precisely that. But the picture, inevitably, is more complicated when it comes to the matter of a human geography of the region, since the 'barrier' is by no means impenetrable and, indeed, is penetrated as a matter of course by all manner of delightful anomalies. I must make it my business in the volume I shall eventually compose from these jottings to explain something of the more intriguing of these.

The Pyrenees, then, are perceived not only as the divide between France and Spain but, with the memory of the Moors in mind, as that between Africa and Europe, with all the complexities of culture, race and language that inevitably festoon such a notion.

When, coming from the north, one stands on the heights at Roncesvalles, with its romantic historical and legendary associations with Count Roland and the *preux chevaliers* of medieval epic, and looks down towards the plain of the Ebro and Spain beyond, one is conscious of a vista of possibilities reaching faraway to the south, to the very portals of Africa itself, where the notion of fearsome heat contrasts dramatically in the mind with the chill of one's still European vantage point. This is much more apparent here, for instance, than is the sense of the Tyrol and Italy from the German side of the Bavarian Alps – perhaps because here one may stand on the heights without scaling any peaks to do so. That is the simple and therefore likely explanation. The fact remains that the character of the region is quite unlike that of any other one may care to name. And although it is not my intention to venture into Spain as such, not on this occasion anyway, it is perhaps worth mentioning that this is a country which is not of Europe in the sense in which France, Prussia – and indeed Bavaria – and England are, belonging as they largely do to more northerly latitudes. Spain looks like an adjunct, not perhaps quite an afterthought, but nevertheless an entity of its own, whose exotic culture and dark history seem to bear out and reinforce this characteristically northern view of her.

However, it is not my intention to fill out my impression of the Pyrenean regions in terms of human history, even were I equipped to do so, which I most decidedly am not. I shall endeavour rather to convey something of the natural character of a mountain range in which peaks and rock formations of dramatic splendour feature spectacularly alongside lakes and streams, forests and meadows of a quieter but equally luminous magnificence. For there is about the region what can only be described as a quality of radiance, which, albeit in the first instance aesthetic, may easily come to seem almost a moral self-assurance. The observation and perception of such self-evident, miraculous beauty – and I recall the green of the Etang de Bethmale, for instance, alongside an equally vivid recollection of the fearsome Pic du Midi de Bigorre... And then, Gavarnie. What words could one find, conceivably, to do justice to Gavarnie? For this is surely one of the most impressive sights the world has to offer, this titanic cirque of concave rock-wall which rises, on the French side, thousands of feet from the valley floor and whose scale, in consequence, has the most profoundly disturbing effect imaginable upon the mind for the way in which it can compel one to contemplate the insect-like insignificance of any one human creature. And yet, truly, the effect of mountains such as these can also be a moral effect which, however disturbing in one sense, may also serve to remind us of our place in a scheme of things which ranges in dimension from the massive formation of the rocks at Gavarnie to comprehend and include at its opposite extreme the human mites we are, for all our pretensions, our self-esteem and our giddy passions...

Chapter Five

Was there, perhaps, just some sense of anticlimax about the Pyrenean excursion and the volume which resulted from it? For the intellectual independence and mental vigour so carefully fostered on Eleanor's behalf by her father and nurtured by the academic disciplines of Cambridge and Miss Clough's tutelage did not make for any easy compliance with the restraints of conventional genteel existence, and, now she had proved herself capable of organising and implementing an initiative which had been rather more than a glorified holiday walking tour, Eleanor was avid for something altogether larger. This next time should take her out of Europe into regions further afield. She was determined to build upon what had already been achieved, to transform herself from the lady excursionist which she knew herself still to be, despite the opinion of the world, into a traveller and explorer in the tradition of such ladies of the past as Mary Wortley Montagu, Harriet Martineau and others.

On the eve of her departure for a brief sojourn with her French cousins in Normandy, Eleanor packed her Herodotus on an impulse. There would be time, at the ancient château in the woods at Le Molay, to discuss these things with the elderly count, her father's cousin, Hubert de Granville, who, first as a soldier and subsequently as a diplomat, had travelled the eastern Mediterranean and Asia Minor over a number of years. Something would be shaped out of all this, she knew. It was the way of things. The stories she recalled hearing narrated with such delight invariably contained within them that grain of life which would reach out into the world of purpose and action. And so in fact it was to prove, for it was from Count Hubert that Eleanor Tew first heard of the Bakhtiari nomads.

★

There is an important sense in which the impulse to travel, besides being a matter of active curiosity, is quite simply an urge to escape the stale constraints of what is only too familiar. From her childhood, when she had pictured imaginary worlds in the patterns of the nursery wallpaper, Eleanor had had the capacity to create space for herself in which it was possible for her to acknowledge an individual identity which, from its earliest years of life, had not always found it easy to comply with the requirements of conformity. She had spoken to her father and godfather of her desire to attain a true and wholly individual independence as a quest for something not easily come by in European societies, and, indeed, over her twenty-odd years of life, she had schooled herself in evasive strategies of her own invention which were designed to smooth a way through moments of awkwardness and embarrassment. With her brothers for instance, a kind of intellectual tact was almost second nature to her, for she loved them both and would not care to have been a cause of smart or humiliation to them. Where moral orthodoxies were concerned, she employed another kind of discretion which depended largely upon verbal strategies of distraction, irony and ambiguity. One of the greatest delights of her Cambridge years had been the realisation that there existed other women, both of her own age as well as more elderly, who, like herself, had found it necessary to develop ploys recognisably similar to her own with the same ends in view,

and it had been something very significantly more than a
mere embellishment to life that there, in Cambridge, in the
company of one's peers, such evasions could be put aside.
For certainly, with life as it was lived at the social level, one
did long for more of that kind of freedom from constraint,
for the possibility of an unself-conscious moral integrity
such as could be enjoyed only in the company of certain
men of rare quality – her father, Doctor Barnes, Professor
Sidgwick at Cambridge, her Uncle Hubert in Normandy,
Nicholas Duvivier all those years ago. Eleanor had often
smiled to herself at the thought of Jane Austen hiding her
manuscript under the cushions, but of late she had found
herself more inclined than ever before to acknowledge that
it was a hiding which was in question. So, what had one to
do, to live a life out of hiding? Presumably any answer to
that would be an individual one: one's space had to be one's
own, not anybody else's.

To travel then, for her, would be to escape. There would
be adventure, discovery, the satisfaction of colourful
achievement that could be used in the cause of a more
independent style of living for women in general. With her
books on Bavaria and the Pyrenees, she had already begun
to build the edifice of that contribution. Any addition to
that would need to be of an altogether more ambitious
kind, to assert an order of capability which should be
recognised and acknowledged as equal to anything a man
might undertake, short of leading a cavalry charge.

Walking in the Bois du Molay with Hubert de Granville,
Eleanor discussed various options…

'…on the understanding, of course, that I was a diplomat pursuing a working career on behalf of France. So any
advice that I may contrive to offer will be coloured by the
fact that I was never a traveller in the sense that you, my
dear, intend to be. Perhaps I should even say "explorer"?'

'If I am to explore, Uncle, it will be in the sense of exploring exotic ways of existence, styles of culture alien to the European rather than charting the physical geography of little known or unknown regions. For I am no surveyor, no cartographer. Neither do I wish to be. My purpose, I think, will be to observe the mores of the world and its sense of values, and in doing so to highlight aspects of our own. Yes, in so far as I have a purpose, that is it.'

'At least, in part?'

'Precisely so.'

The old count eyed her gravely, then went on in his beautiful, ruminative French, 'but you will observe with respect, will you not?'

'Most certainly. That is not in question.'

'Your rebuke is to the point, my dear. No, no. For you see, as a working diplomat it was my duty to act as the agent of a policy, a policy of power and colonisation. And since we French colonised our empire by cultural means far more consciously, I think, than you English ever conceived possible, there is a fine irony, do you not agree, in the fact that there are now black and yellow men in the world who speak excellent French, a fact which simply and unequivocally confirms the success of that policy? I do envy you, my dear, to be able to go wherever you shall go unshackled by the dictates and protocols of a metropolitan office back in your own country. You have the opportunity to be as unprejudiced an observer as it is possible to be. Like Herodotus, you shall go to see because you want to know.'

'Herodotus is a good example, Uncle. I cherish him myself.'

'So. Let us consider then, in rather more specific terms, where you shall make for first and what kind of society might prove the most enlightening. Mountains you have done. Now, perhaps, you should turn your hand to people—'

'I adore mountains, and the lonely places of the world draw me irresistibly—'

'True, this I appreciate. But people count for more than places. You must know this. Or you should.'

'I have to confess that I find most people of our own kind irksome and too frequently disappointing.'

'Because you disturb them? Ladies are not supposed to think as sharply as you do, eh?'

'Very likely.'

'Then how do you imagine you might fare in the kind of society – of which there are not a few – where the women are effectively no more than active beasts of burden to their men, peacock men whose pride in those male virtues essential to the security and survival of the group or tribe is likely to strike you, my dear, as… irksome, if not positively absurd?'

'I shall observe these things, Uncle. I have no intention of becoming a part of them myself. But you have something in mind, I think, to speak thus?'

'It occurred to me that, of those societies with which I am familiar, the one which could be of greatest interest to your purposes as I understand them could well be a nomadic one, as nomads are in virtually every way as far removed from us as it is possible to be.'

'I am intrigued, Uncle. Do continue.'

'Very well. To begin with, you must imagine a life lived constantly on the move, from one day, one week, one month, one year to the next. The sole purpose of this life is to safeguard and maintain the health and well-being of the flocks which represent the estate and *raison d'être* of the tribe. The route out and back has been determined since time immemorial and involves the crossing of several mountain ranges as well as rivers, through snow and ice and through spring flood water. There is a collective tribal memory which operates within a dimension positively Old

Testament in its style of perception. For instance: "And the father of our people came out of the fastness of the southern mountains in ancient times. His seed were as numerous as the rocks on the mountains, and his people prospered". And so on, that kind of thing.'

'Of whom do you speak, Uncle?'

'Of the Bakhtiari nomads of south-western Persia.'

'Do continue.'

'The whole undertaking is a heroic adventure that leads nowhere for, at the end of the journey there is... nothing other than an immense resignation. The tribal mentality is, you must understand, as opposite to your own as is possible. I wonder, my dear, if you could come to terms with that?'

'A challenge, Uncle?'

'No, no, my dear. I should not wish to inveigle you into anything, let alone anything of such moment as this would be. The planning of such an expedition alone would take a considerable amount of time and trouble. For it would have to be approached with great care and circumspection, as all kinds of diplomatic and international ramifications and niceties would necessarily present themselves.'

'In due course, then, perhaps, Uncle. But for the moment, tell me more of the Bakhtiari.'

'The end of the journey, then, is marked by the final test at the crossing of the Bazuft river, by now swollen with three months' melt water. All – tribesmen and women, flocks, pack animals – are exhausted. Today the young become men; their strength will guarantee the survival of the herd and the tribal family. For the old it is the end. If they cannot manage the river crossing, they simply remain behind and die. It is the end of the journey and there is no longer any place for them. Such is the nomad custom and as such it is accepted, in resignation and equanimity. There is, in my view, a fine and simple dignity to that, a kind of properly stoic answer to the biggest question of all, the one which bedevils us quite beyond what is reasonable. Do you recall Vigny's wolf, *qui meurt sans jeter un cri*? I've always admired that. Having soldiered a bit myself, I can see the appeal of it. And, besides, there is something worth pondering, is there not, in the thought that the warrior aristocrat on the one hand and the primitive nomad herdsman on the other appear to have come to the same conclusion over life's most portentous question?'

'Nothing in his life became him like the leaving it.'

'But naturally. Shakespeare usually does have the last word in these matters. But you, my dear. How would it be for you, do you imagine, were you to find yourself face to face with death?'

'Uncle, I have never even begun to consider it, although perhaps we do allow ourselves, generally I mean, to be excessively preoccupied by the thought of it.'

'And do you find this surprising?'

'Not in itself. What surprises me is what people are capable of allowing themselves to believe. What appals me is the way in which the cultural evolution of man has thrown up such massive, institutionalised orthodoxies whose purpose it is to perpetuate their own interest by bolstering illusion.'

'Ah! But perhaps they do not see it in quite this way! And, besides, do you not expect a little too much of our poor benighted species? We may talk glibly of progress and of the advance of science and knowledge, but we are the children of a human past fraught with superstitious terror, a terror born of the knowledge of our vulnerability in a fearsome world. And one hundred years ago there were those who had begun to appreciate and understand this – did you know there was a Théophile de Granville – oh, yes! – who accompanied Bougainville on his travels? That exploratory curiosity, that fascination with other modes of existence before the extension of imperial power and colonisation came into play – that was a truly Greek thing, it seems to me. One should look carefully at certain French explorers and philosophers of the last century.'

'And yet you yourself, Uncle, led a life of active involvement in the affairs of France.'

'True, my dear. I can only say that circumstances determined it should be thus and not otherwise. Now, however, I enjoy my moment of contemplation in the knowledge that my duty was discharged.'

'Like the Sieur de Montaigne?'

'My dear, you flatter me. But a bit like, perhaps. I should say, though, that I prefer my own home to the château de Montaigne. Infinitely.'

★

In 1879, as preparations for what Eleanor had come to think of – xenophonically, in her private phrase – as her Persian expedition neared completion, news reached the Tew family in Leamington Spa that Captain William Tew, serving with Lord Chelmsford's army in South Africa, had been killed in action on the slopes of Mount Isandhlwana, expertly assegaied and ripped open as a mark of regard by an enemy of precisely his own ilk, in order that his cheery warrior's soul might be released heavenwards to find its just deserts there. Willie had died, it was later determined, defending a hopeless position with a bayonet team; the ferocity and stubborn character of the defence was inferred by observers from the number of gutted Zulu corpses in their vicinity. Willie and his men had been overwhelmed quite simply by weight of numbers in an assault on their position whose speed, timing and direction had been wholly unanticipated by a slow-witted, complacent British command. It was understood that there was a question of posthumous commendation.

Once beyond the initial shock, the ravaging grief whose onset knows no resistance, Theophilus Tew, in the fastness of his private sanctum, pondered the matter. This, then, this gory end, the consequence of a commander's ineptitude, was what it had amounted to – Willie's life: all the little-boy rumbustiousness, the anxious emulations of his senior twin who, fortunately, had been elsewhere in South Africa at that time, the partying, the moustachioed dandyism, the pride in his swordsmanship, the unassuming fearlessness, the noise, the unfailing good humour. Theophilus wept bitterly for the waste of his son's precious life. Just this once, he promised himself, he would allow his grief free rein, as was only proper where the death of a dear son was in question. After that had run its course, though, there should be nothing if not a grave dignity. For there would have to be public rituals of commemoration and there was Charlotte to be consoled, so far as that might be possible.

Charlotte would be a problem. The self-indulgent sentimentality she had cultivated over the long recent years of their married life would have a heyday, he realised. There would be paroxysms, most likely, of exhibitionistic grief. The thought revolted him; indeed, he acknowledged, most things about Charlotte now revolted him. For this reason he determined to make a conscious effort to preserve a decorous distance between them, an effort which, he calculated, would be abetted by her aversion to his views on virtually everything, by her mindless devotion to religion and the cultivation of a gratuitous, genteel notion of decorum. Theophilus had known, knew humble men and women more mannerly than such a lady, although this was something Charlotte could never have understood, immured as she was within the odious values she had chosen to espouse. This sudden upsurge of aversion, after years of complaisant conniving on his part, took him quite by surprise by its intensity. Momentarily, Theophilus experienced a fear amounting almost to panic at the thought of the precise nature of the other man within himself.

But he would talk himself back into equanimity with Eleanor for, over the years, they had found a coded style of exchange in which to discuss such matters. Barnes, too, would be helpful in his tactful way. Theophilus knew, even in his present desolation of spirit, that he was fortunate indeed to have the confidence and affection of two such fine individuals. The thought crossed his mind, almost casually, that if Barnes had not been such an inveterate old bachelor, he and Eleanor might well have made a fine match. Then, in the briefest moment of absolute clarity, he understood the deepest thing about his old friend and marvelled at the selflessness of the man, saw too the point of the pleasures he knew to be bought in London, Paris and Venice. It had quite simply stared him in the face for years. And in all the sadness of his grief for William, Theophilus was moved, cheered and sustained by the truth his private pain had made manifest to him. By his death, in his dying, William had made his contribution to matters of still living significance. Theophilus resolved that, somehow or other, Barnes should be tacitly apprised of what he, his old friend, knew and understood of his worth and the enhanced regard in which he should be held from then on. What might then ensue… But that, Theophilus acknowledged, was out of his hands. For where Eleanor was concerned… Her father, with wry self-deprecation, could allow only that the emotional life of his favourite daughter was a complete mystery to him, that although he knew her to enjoy the society of gentlemen, the high spirits and jollity and urbane good humour of elegant social life – as indeed what normal healthy young woman would not – and here Theophilus once again recalled the Regency delights of his own early manhood and allowed himself a moment's execration of the fashionable, self-conscious anxieties of the present day – he had to admit that, where deeper feelings were concerned, where the matter of any emotionally-based commitment came into question, he knew his daughter not at all.

★

'Dearly beloved, we are gathered here today, in this parish church of All the Saints, to commemorate and give thanks to Almighty God for the life of Captain William Francis de Granville Tew, who died a soldier's death in pursuit of his military duty against a heathen race in a distant land. I shall not speak in great detail of William, whom we all knew and loved, for, although we must and surely do rejoice that he is now with his Father in Heaven, this cannot but be an occasion also of mourning and grief at the loss we sustain in his passing from us.

'There is, though, an important sense in which William's life, as well as the manner of his dying, was enviably all of a piece. Those of us who are in a position to do so will recall his time as an active, energetic young man at Rugby School – never a scholar, William, but one who, much more importantly, threw himself with energy and vigour and enthusiasm into the life of the community. One may recall, also, his pride in his army commission, his regard for his regiment and his fellow officers, his pride in his swordsmanship, a legitimate pride, one feels, born of his admiration for the skills of those who instructed him in the use of arms. And how fitting that the sword, the weapon of the gentleman warrior throughout the ages, should have been the weapon in the use of which William's excellence has been acknowledged, whether in the *salle d'armes* – in practice and in regimental sport – or in earnest on the field of battle itself.

'Now, William's sword rests here for him, upon his coffin, as is befitting: a badge of rank properly borne, a symbol of honour and obligation discharged unflinchingly in the terrible face of a savage, remorseless enemy whose gods, whosoever they may be, one can only shudder to imagine.

'For this was a fine English gentleman, a proud chevalier in the legendary tradition of his knightly French ancestors, a faithful paladin of the One, True and Christian God...'

Beside the human wreck that had been her mother, Eleanor Tew listened, expressionless. With the family around and behind her in the congregation which filled the capacious, vaulted edifice of the parish church of Leamington Spa, she was aware of particular presences: Rachel and her husband, Mr Collingdale; Gwendolen and Jemima with Mary Beaufoy; Frederick, granite-faced, accompanied by a grey-haired gentleman of distinguished military aspect whom she recognised, with something of a shock, as Nicholas Duvivier. Revolted by the words and sentiments of the clergyman, she recalled that the Zulu mutilation of an enemy's corpse was a mark of regard for a doughty adversary, whose fighting soul, thus released, should find its due place in the heaven of warriors, wherever that may be. She was aware too of her father and Doctor Barnes, both ageing gentlemen now, she saw. It was as if the glimpse of Duvivier had brought home to her something – almost, as it were, for the first time – of the passing of the years. Eleanor fixed her gaze upon the profile of her father, sensed the sadness in him and perceived also the dignity. And intuitively, through her closeness to him, she knew something of the harrowing disappointment of his relations with her mother, knew also that his feelings at that moment could not but be akin to her own.

But her Persian expedition should contribute to the moral rehabilitation of the family by bringing additional consequence to the name of Tew. This purpose too should be added to the complex of her intentions in mounting it.

She made up her mind to be gone from England as soon as was decently possible.

From Eleanor Tew to Theophilus Tew, Esquire, 1880

Dearest Father,

We have now put Europe well and truly behind us with, two days ago, a final sighting of the southernmost extremity of the Italian peninsula. We are now well past the volcanic islands of that region and steam our way steadily eastwards towards that end of the Mediterranean and Port Said, whence I shall travel overland across Arabia and eventually down as far as the Strait of Hormuz. My route continues thence into Persia itself by way of the south-west as planned. Xenophonically, I do declare!

You may imagine, I think, the thrill of exultation it gives me to write these words. For I had long since decided, even before my Pyrenean excursion was completed and published, that my next major enterprise should take me significantly further afield and into the world at large. As I contemplate this prospect now, with all it entails, I cannot but quail somewhat at the character of the undertaking. You, of all people, will appreciate, however, that this is no mere ladylike shrinking from the terrible prospect of a reality which threatens to be overwhelming, but, rather, my response to a perception of the world – renewed by all manner of unfamiliarities since I sailed from England – as an awesomely beautiful and terrifyingly strange habitat. For we all carve out our cosy little niche, do we not? We find, if we are fortunate, occupation of significance and value to carry us through life usefully and serviceably, but in doing so we forgo the raw experience of so much that awaits us in the way of wonder and mystery and even salutary terror. If only we could view this, our earth, from way out in the cosmos, from way beyond the moon, say, I like to imagine that what should strike us about it in the first instance would be a kind of radiant beauty, akin, perhaps, to that of a diamond brilliant against the black of velvet. And indeed, one day, who knows? By whatever means. However, I draw renewed moral strength from my apprehensions as we forge into the unknown, as the prodigious excitement of the venture possesses me. Dear Father, I know from what you recounted to me of your own early travels that you will understand these thoughts of mine. I hope to pen them in due course somewhat more exactly into the words which will eventually constitute the published version of my Persian expedition...

So, I venture into a new phase and mode of existence and who could possibly know where this may lead? At all events, I shall endeavour to remain in correspondence with you, sir, as with dear Anna Rowlandson, whose Belgravia address you have. Now that the appalling pain of our loss of dear William has begun, with the passing of time, to abate somewhat, or at least to lose something of its initial bitterness, I trust that my decision to abide by my previous intention to journey beyond Europe will not be construed by yourself, or indeed anyone else whose good opinion I value, as an abandoning of responsibilities which ought properly to feature more imperatively in my scheme of things. For, despite the protestations of Mamma, about which I think you know, it is nothing of the kind. Of course I still weep for my dear brother and for all those who are involved in the pain of his loss. But William was a soldier and for him the possibility of death must always have been a very real thing. With the wisdom of a retrospective nous so dearly purchased, I gladly acknowledge my admiration for the equanimity, the cheery insouciance of those of the twins' brother officers, including of *course most particularly poor dear George Rowlandson, whom it was my privilege to meet, knowing – as I now infer this – something of that special awareness in which they went about their military occasions. In time, I trust, we shall warm to our fond recollections of William and to the proud manner of his dying, even as we never cease to mourn over the fact that he is no more.*

Now, though, as I picture you and Doctor Barnes together in the den at Clarendon Crescent, the thought that a few short paces from this table at which I write will suffice to bring me on deck, where I can view the stars in the eastern sky in order to take cognisance of what lies behind me and what before, is an inexpressibly vital thought and one which will not be quelled simply, come what may. One begins to discern something of what the ancient notion of the god Dionysus was about. Oh, as always, the sanity of the Greeks!

Dearest Father, you are ever in my thoughts, as I trust I am in yours. And whatever may be in store for me as I pursue my purposes on this expedition, I shall draw strength and courage from my sense of your interest and understanding, as also from the perception that the fact of geographical distance is as nothing when set against the enduring power of what unites us.

And so, to the desert! The wilderness. Such a biblical term, one feels, and yet, not inappropriate, since the ways and practices of these primitive regions can surely have changed little in two thousand years or so. What a moral lift the thought induces! In my imagination I reach out in anticipation of a certain destiny which will free me from all that is blinkered and jejune in the fashionable notion, the fad of progress. For it is in the wilderness, I know, that I shall come close to what is the essence of the human condition. Do you, therefore, Father, bear with me in my search for whatever I may find in that place...

Part Two
Sam Webster

Chapter One

Nick's letter arrived at his French retreat just a matter of days before Sam prepared to set off back for London and home. All in all, it had been a fruitless summer in the Pyrenees, as his new novel, intended as a follow-up to the prizewinning *Ticklebeast* of three years back, was obstinately refusing to turn into anything in which he could begin to find any real interest as yet. In fact, he could not but admit, Sam had used every evasion known to literary man that summer to put off the moment when he would have to admit to himself that this, most likely, was nothing more than yet another of the false starts which, in due course, would litter the shelves of his workroom back in Kew, along with other similar packages of handwritten A4 paper, abandoned floppy disks and all the detritus of the professional writer's frustration with his trade.

So Nick's letter was especially welcome, Sam told himself. And, indeed, it exuded a kind of urbane, manic delight at what he, Nick, the writer, was about to impart to his old friend. Nick, as he pointed out himself, had carried it off. There was to be a series of programmes, of a documentary-historical character, on travellers. Who the travellers were to be was still open to negotiation but in principle it was on. And Sam was to have a slot, possibly even two. The name of Sam Webster, on mention, had elicited instant, delighted approval. There had been at least one other chap present at the meeting at Enterprise House who had recalled the piece on the transhumant shepherds of Provence that Sam had made for, was it Channel Four? Two or three years back? People had been most positive about the whole thing, most positive. We are therefore, as it were, in business.

In Business. A thing they had written together, he and Nick, for Footlights at Cambridge thirty years ago. Now, it seemed, Nick found his most potent gratification in the executive power his position at Independent Television Enterprises gave him to cast such crumbs as this – admittedly a substantial crumb – before those who preferred the actual making, like Sam himself, though at university they had both been 'writers'. But the whirligig of time brings out, inexorably, those inevitabilities latent in each unique and inimitable configuration of character and personality, and the glitter of power and influence and the kind of opulence they bring with them are not to be denied. And neither are they to be scorned and dismissed, Sam admonished himself in anticipation of some such knee-jerk inclination, for they belong with those who make things possible; they go with a kind of active involvement.

Sam pottered amiably about his Pyrenean cottage, closing up for the end of summer. Since his marriage had finally ended, just prior to the publication of *Ticklebeast* three years previously, he had learned to be alone, to be his own man, to treasure the idiosyncrasies of the writer's solitude. Thus, when the society of sympathetic friends made its claim, when a liaison was offered, these things were the more to be appreciated now that it was possible to engage with them on his own terms. Present problems with the novel he was attempting to work on would resolve themselves sooner or later, he knew, and the alternatives to a happy optimism were too awful to contemplate.

Now the colours of the countryside around were just perceptibly beginning to soften: there was the beginning of a mellow quality to things which, to him, had a particular insistence about it. Time to get back to London, it hinted, to get handwritten summer notes into at least some sort of shape on the word processor in Kew. In the distance the snow-capped peaks and ridges of the Pyrenees remained, as always, immutable. Immutably there. Mountains, he thought, gave you a perspective on it all; that was the thing about them, with their reminder of unimaginably huge tracts of time, so huge that the very notion of age in human terms became virtually insignificant. The view of the mountains from the old Pyrenean shepherd's cottage could not have changed in the hundreds of years the house had been standing there. But in terms of mountain time... Sam secured a shutter, carted out the rubbish and swept out the kitchen, enjoying his thoughts as he did so.

Nick Hopley. Once, for a brief while, Nik Hopley. Now well on the way to being Nicholas Hopley, of Independent Television Enterprises, one whose pronouncements on broadcasting policy, on the relations between government and the media – contentious stuff, this – were quoted and attentively measured and assessed. One deft in the manipulation of ambiguity and uncertainty, an artist of the non-committal, the grandest master of evasive strategies. Sam recalled, as from a great distance, their undergraduate delight in that particular kind of cleverness. Ironic appreciation of the deliberately anodyne. But it had long since become deadly serious, all that, where Nick was concerned. Always a manipulator, he had made effective use of a special skill, but somewhere the irony went out of it all; the sense of absurdity, and with it the fun got lost.

So much for the lesson satire teaches, but then perhaps he himself, Sam thought, had been the one of the two of them who had never grown up. For pride in a book well written or a film well made was as nothing much, surely, without the power to ensure these things reached a public? In some way, though, that was not the crux of the matter and Sam knew it was not. Anyway, he would turn his mind to the question of the travellers and begin to think it all out in rather more detail as he made his way back north to the Channel.

There was to be a number of writers involved, Nick had made it clear, and the first stage in the project would be for each of them – some half a dozen names established as authors or makers of documentary films – to put together a scenario for the series that would concern the individual contribution plus a larger notion of how the series might look in the round. So, it seemed to Sam, that there should be some principle of unity and continuity, perhaps contained within a title for the whole thing, some form of words which would give an identity to what was as yet merely the notion of 'a series on travel Quent's been hankering after for ages, for one'. The afterthought was typical. Quentin Rodgers was an inventive, brilliant, resourceful young producer only a few years out of university but already well on his way to what would most probably be great distinction. But as yet he had won only recognition and plaudits. The great prizes would surely come his way in due course, but they had not done so yet so, naturally, Hopley, predictable as always, would hedge his bets. So, 'Quent... for one'. A tiny qualification to reflect a whole world.

Possibly something along those lines would give suitable substance to the idea of the series? If such a thing could be found. Sam pondered and got nowhere, but that was, after all, simply an aspect of the trade. Something would present itself eventually, he knew, one way or another. It was a question of being on the lookout for it. The idea of something from Marco Polo, for instance, echoing down the centuries, might be worth considering, something to suggest that the lure of travel was a perennial thing. One could do a nice historical montage from maps and prints to illustrate the fascination of the business over time, but then the series must not give the impression of being an historical affair: it was to be of contemporary relevance, pertaining to the variety of interests physical, cultural and human that the world had to offer in the here and now. Sam loved the idea of strangeness and familiarity, of similarity within difference, of distances historical, cultural and physical at the heart of which one came across what was instantly recognisable to the common human view. And there were of course all kinds of interesting anomalies – people whose moral positives were villainous by Western standards, people whose languages did not operate in sentences or even in sounds manageable to voices attuned to Western modes of utterance. Giles La Haye had done some work on the language aspect, Sam recalled. He might give him a ring at the School of Oriental and African Studies, assuming he might be back in London in a while, for the beginning of the academic year in October.

For travel celebrates these things, belonging as it does to those who possess enough in the way of interest and opportunity to want to go and see for themselves. Then there were other motives, such as escape from what was intolerable, the assertion of self, political imperatives... There were various purposes in question: it was not a straightforward thing, not at all, but it was an incontrovertible fact that, generation after generation, people took the most appalling discomforts in their stride and were, besides, simply not discouraged by hardship, disease, danger. Among his own friends, there was at least one, Sam knew, who for a period in his life had been accustomed to sleeping with a loaded revolver beneath his pillow. For most people, though, packaged tourism was the nearest they ever got to any of this. And what an improvement in the common lot that represented, anyway. One would not wish to knock the holiday industry and besides, ITE would never allow anything of that sort. Nick would be on to that in a flash.

There were various ways in which one could approach this project, Sam reflected. One could, for instance, do a historical-chronological treatment with a look at the Renaissance origins, although there had of course been great pilgrimages before that. The road to Santiago was a case in point; he recalled an impressive exhibition of photographs – of landmarks along the way to Santiago de Compostela – which he had looked over out of curiosity on a brief visit to Lübeck recently. A mention perhaps, on second thoughts. Or something rather more than a mere passing reference? To highlight the difference of purpose and intention between the medieval pilgrimage, a strictly soul-saving investment, and a more modern, post-Renaissance curiosity in things worldly for their own intrinsic fascination.

Or there were mountains, jungles, deserts, other kinds of wilderness, each in its turn representing a different kind of challenge. There were soldiers, Sam knew, who were specialists in survival in all kinds of difficult terrain. Some advice from that quarter, an opinion or two, could be helpful.

On the south bank of the great River Loire at Saumur, where he stopped off for a hard-earned driver's lunch just round the corner from the famous cavalry school, Sam filled a cheap French exercise book with notes: there always came a point beyond which he found it impossible to retain every idea without losing one or two in the process, and he was loath to miss out on anything which might be of use, whether in itself or as a lead to something further but as yet unforeseen.

Sam eyed the great river as it flowed westwards to the sea, took in quite casually the presence of a little cluster of anglers on the far bank just down river from where the bridge, to his right, threw its gracious span of elegant arches across the water. The thought occurred to him that Charles Lytton's *Eminent Adventurers* might be worth a browse through. He knew exactly where it was to be found among his books, in the small green bookcase in the guest bedroom at Haverfield Gardens, an old hardback bound in green cloth with a burgundy label and faded gold lettering on the spine, a book untouched for ages but not forgotten, a series of rather waspish, debunking biographical sketches of figures of erstwhile household stature where 'adventure' had been concerned; little-boy heroes, one might have said. It had come, seventy years ago now, at the end of an era, at one of those moments when the cracks in the façade of straight heroism had just begun to show. Lytton, being just the man to savour those more equivocal quirks of personality which impel certain people to particular kinds of action, had quite deliberately widened a few of those cracks in order, in the voyeuristic style of his kind, to peer in at them and snigger at what he found there and, of course, to invite the knowing connivance of his reader at the same time. The very book was an act of inadequacy in its own right, but there were some good, perceptive things in it, Sam recalled, nevertheless. Almost in conscious parody of himself, he wrote down the title in his exercise book, then strolled back to his modest Peugeot and drove out of Saumur over the bridge and up the N147. He would soon be in Normandy, which was almost home.

Chapter Two

Back in London, Sam picked up the threads of a busy, somewhat fragmented existence. There were messages on the answerphone, mail, a number of faxes to be dealt with, a request from his ex-wife to ring her at home after the twenty-fifth – today was the twenty-seventh. He remembered to look out the copy of *Eminent Adventurers* which had been just where he remembered it, he left it out for a browse later, when he got the chance.

He had lunch, more or less on the hoof, with Julian Rosenberg, the literary agent who handled his work. Chablis and crab sandwiches in a noisy pub in Putney. Sam broached the Hopley project.

'Nick Hopley? Shifty sod. You want to watch him.'

'I was at Cambridge with him. Know him pretty well.'

'So what? You know how the style of television has changed. Whatever they may say in their public pronouncements, however they may protest their undying devotion to a traditional notion of quality broadcasting, there is a new philosophy abroad. They call it getting "value for money". What it boils down to in effect, as far as you are concerned anyway, is screwing the writers. So I don't care if you shared a sleeping bag with Hopley at the Edinburgh Festival twenty-five years ago or whatever! Anyway, I'll handle it for you as usual. We must look for some kind of a tactical advantage – a bit of a lever. I'll think about that when I get the official description of the project with an indication of what your contribution is going to be. Over the signature of the programme controller. Designated as such.'

It was a timely reminder, for Sam, of the milieu of the word trade – he was well and truly back in the Smoke. He was glad that he had agreed to meet Julian, sharp and clever and energetic as he was. A real friend of irrepressible resource. Sam recalled that his son Joe had mentioned in a letter about his having met up with Emma Rosenberg, one of Julian's several daughters, in a May Ball party back in June.

That evening, over a dram of the Edradour, he leafed through the Lytton book of Victorian explorers, for such they had been for the most part. Doughty, Stanley, Speke, Burton, Kinglake, a couple more. Now Burton had been a man to reckon with – not in the Hopley sense but as a human phenomenon in his day – a misfit bursting with an energy for which English society had been quite unable to find a use, and who had, therefore, taken himself off elsewhere, in impatience, no doubt, and contempt. Then there was the Catholic wife, who burnt his manuscripts because she could not face the truth of what he had to tell. But there is the translation of *The Thousand and One Nights* – as fitting a memorial as any, one might say.

It was typical of Lytton, Sam mused, to have chosen 'adventurers' for his title, with the possibility it implied of louche connotation. Lytton had it there, every way. Sam had to acknowledge the verbal nous of the man, even as he noted with irritated distaste the sly innuendo of the literary queen in the paradox of his title. At all events, though, it was alive still, his dusty old book, untouched for years in the guest room bookcase. Delighted with himself and his thoughts, Sam put out the lights and went to bed.

★

They gathered, the project team, for the first time in a small conference room at ITE on the South Bank, overlooking the site of Wanamaker's Globe Theatre. Urbanely presiding, handing out chewy sweets, was Nick Hopley, Controller of Documentary Features, with responsibility for all sorts of other things; with a secretary, 'Vanessa darling'; Quentin Rodgers in ratty old jeans beautifully laundered, gold bracelet and a pullover top probably worth several hundred pounds; and four writers including Sam. Turning to his immediate neighbour as he sat down, Sam instantly recognised this to be Geoff Hayward, a pallid, lank-haired, chain-smoking ghost of a fellow, whom he recalled as one of the sharpest, most iconoclastic wits of their joint Cambridge day, one who had lived by night and slept by day.

'Lo, Sam,' said this individual; it was as though they had last met the day before yesterday rather than twenty-five years ago or whatever it was. It transpired that he had spent much of that intervening time up in the Arctic Circle; 'not quite doing the Dead-Eye Dick but almost, you know? A moose or two, the odd caribou...'

They sat round one of those tables designed so that everyone round it could see everyone else.

'Just a preliminary, informal sort of do,' said Hopley easily, by way of opening the proceedings, 'by way of a bit of a start. Actually meeting each other, having a natter to sort a few things out. Quentin's very excited about the whole thing, aren't you, Quent?'

'Guardedly, Nick, guardedly. I mean, we'll be wanting to see what transpires, won't we? But yes, I am. The idea is one I've wanted to have a real go at for ages.'

'We'll come to that in a moment, Quent, if I might just make a small preliminary point?'

'Sure, Nick. Do.'

'Thank you, Quent. The point is this. There are four writers here; Sam Webster, Geoff Hayward, Nigel Wheatley, Martin Saggers. You are all writers of very different kinds, that's deliberate, and – and this is the point – there should be six of you, but two of the other possibles can't make it and we're still waiting for responses from some of the others we had in mind. So, we should like to ask you to put together your own scenario on the theme. Subject names, for instance. Do we want to do Burton? Somebody did him a few years ago; can't remember who. Do we want a chronological sequence? Shall we stick to English names? If we do can we include Stanley if we want to? How far back do we start? Do we want something separate by way of an introduction? And so on and so on. Also, we thought we might canvass your opinion on writers to make up the six, or perhaps there are those of you who might care to undertake two names rather than just one, or would that spread contention, strife, jealousy and all the rest of it, ha, ha!'

'Six parts, is it?'

'Provisionally. Certainly no more.'

'How long?'

'Effectively one hour apiece.'

'Do we feature?'

'Could be discussed. If you want to, and if we think you look good enough on screen. Quent's thing, that.'

'Fair enough'

'Nigel's okay, of course. We've all seen his *Back of Beyond*, and Mart, as king of the political thriller and well-known public personality. Sam and Geoff we'll deal with in due course as need arises, although, Sam, I seem to recall – and I'm sorry I haven't checked this out – that you did appear with your Provençal shepherds, am I right?'

'You are.'

'Thank you, Quent. And now, gentlemen… ah, coffee! Vanessa, darling, do you think you might do the honours? Thank you, sweetie. Now, where was I? Oh, yes. Material. Names of subjects. I know Quentin has a few thoughts on this, but let's see what you've all come up with so far, shall we? Nigel?'

'Fawcett. Or perhaps Peter Fleming and Fawcett. Love to do that.'

'Terrific. I like that. What about you, Quent?'

'Possibilities, Nick. Decidedly. "The Case of the Vanishing Colonel", eh?'

'Lovely! Why not? Brilliant, Quent. Absolutely brilliant!'

For all Hopley's gush, good humour spread through the gathering at the undoubtedly attractive quality of Wheatley's enthusiastic, purposeful gambit and the deft and stylish way in which Rodgers had picked up on it. Nigel Wheatley, Sam recalled. *Notes From the Back of Beyond.* A young social anthropologist who had contrived to turn his postgraduate fieldwork into a good-humouredly comical, self-deprecating account of the hazards and vicissitudes of such undertakings. The book had sold very well and had recently appeared in Penguin. A fair-haired young man, expensively attired in Prince of Wales check and wearing an expression of ironic amusement on his face at the unfailing absurdity of the world and its denizens, Wheatley had the bright, blue-eyed poise and confidence and, most likely, also, the unshakeable equanimity of one whose superlative intelligence could simply never be in question. Sam liked the look of him.

'Sam?'

'Not entirely sure yet, Nick. But Kinglake? Kingsley possibly even better? Probably a Victorian, possibly Africa, possibly a lady.'

'Goo-od, sounds promising. Are we going to contrive to cover different continents, do you think? Would that be good? I mean, under the umbrella of something like, say, "This World of Ours"? Only a suggestion!' Nick held up both hands as though to ward off objections.

'Possibilities, Nick. Definitely worth considering.'

'Thank you, Quent. Geoff?'

'Iceland, Nick. William Morris's *Travels in Iceland* in the 1870s. I might make something of that, I think. It's my part of the world.'

'Good, Geoff. I like that. Nice contrast with the other two. Keep in touch with Quent over this, won't you? Martin?'

Martin Saggers, small, hatchet-faced, expensively tailored in pinstripes and silk, spoke in ringing tones that signalled the confidence of a certain kind of wealth and success. To Sam, listening, the anomaly of his presence at the gathering was confirmed in the tenor of that voice. There were, of course, writers and writers – notoriously disparate, unclubbable, perversely individualistic, contrary loners for the most part. This man had made a business-man's fortune from a certain kind of predictable formula thriller in the fashionable, contemporary, political dimension. Sam would not be beholden to Hopley for bracketing him with such a man, and he knew without having to enquire that Hayward would feel the same. Nigel Wheatley, so inimitably his own and much younger man, probably could not care less. And that, Sam decided, should be the answer, by dint of necessity. But he was intrigued and curious...

'An Empire man, I thought, Nicholas. Thesiger, perhaps, or Speke—'

'Thesiger?' Hayward interrupted. 'Thesiger's his own man. Not the sovereign's, despite his service, and certainly not anyone else's. That's the whole point about him. He chose to make his life among the simplest folk because he couldn't abide his own kind! Unless of course you're thinking of that clown who lost an army at Isandhlwana?'

'I take exception to that.'

'Tough'.

'Gentlemen, if you please...'

At the head of the table Hopley was poised to pour himself on these troubled waters.

'All right. Martin, we'll think this through. You keep in touch, okay? Because I really do think we've made a cracking start. We've got a mystery from Nigel; possibly a lady from Sam; the northern thing from Geoff and an Empire man, or whatever, from Martin. Supposing, for instance, one began with Fawcett and used his disappearance to raise the question of why people get up to this kind of thing at all? I like what we've got so far, I really do. What about you, Quent?'

'Oh certainly, Nick. Good stuff.'

'So, thank you for coming, and we'll keep in touch.'

People began to move, to stand and stretch, gather up notes and papers. Saggers left first, without a word to anyone. Sam squared up to Hayward, who blocked his jab to the ribs and came back with a left hook to the jaw, as of old.

'How about a drink and sandwich?'

'Good thinking, Ticklebeast. The National's just down the road, and I'm going to the Stoppard matinee this afternoon anyway.'

'Right, then. We're off. Cheers, Nick.'

'Cheers, fellows.' Hopley looked as though he might be on the point of saying more, but changed his mind.

'Be in touch.'

'Sure, Sam. Be in touch.'

At the National Theatre, provided with claret and a pile of sandwiches, Hayward knocked back a quick preliminary scotch, lit a fresh cigarette from the stub of the last one and eyed Sam.

'And what, then, do you imagine that that berk Hopley is up to, inviting that sod Saggers into all this? I mean, for Christ's sake, do you really think he knew anything about Thesiger? Speke might have been about his level, I should have thought, if that's not an insult to Speke, but, hah!'

'Geoff,' Sam chewed a mouthful of pâté sandwich and sipped Saint Emilion. 'Let us consider this as one of those intriguing anomalies that life is sometimes good enough to throw up for our delectation—'

'That's how you see it, is it?'

'Geoff, one is a writer, when all is said and done. One must be grateful for whatever may come one's way, for the occasional illumination of some obscure feature of life's great tapestry—'

'Stop pissing about, Sam. You always were a pisser about!'

'I know, Geoff. It's just the way I think—'

'And bugger the mock humility too! Look! Don't you feel put out, if that's not too strong a term, to be bracketed with that pinstriped little turd? Without wishing to make too much of it, and all that, and stand on one's doodah, but even so... Well, don't you?'

'I do see what you mean, Geoff. Of course I do. And I could feel as you do if I allowed myself to but, as it is, I'm more intrigued than anything, I must say. What is afoot, I ask myself; what can be... well, you know, up? You know what Hopley's like. People don't change, do they? No indeed. My guess is that there's some sort of strategic thing here, something to do with TV politics that probably has nothing much to do with individual contributors.'

'Who appear to count for very little then? One writer's much the same as the next, eh?'

'Geoff, where have you been these last few years? Don't you know this? But I forgot – you've been away for ages, haven't you? How long did you spend on the reindeer book? Which I thought was marvellous incidentally, I really did. The Thubron of the North, I said to myself when I read it. But go on, sorry.'

'It took me five years. But not all up in Lappland. I had a stint in Stockholm teaching at the university, then I borrowed a friend's *stuga* in the archipelago for six months while he was in Provence and did most of the writing there.'

'But you did know that Saggers was one of the brains behind the publicity campaign which got this government returned at the last election, I assume?'

'Of course I knew. I mean, that's the point, isn't it? You wouldn't want to be thought to be in cahoots with a thing like that, surely?'

'Geoff, the only answer is to be your own man. Which reminds me. I must tell my agent Saggers is involved. He won't be doing it for peanuts and we might be able to screw some more money out of Nick, see?'

'Christ, literary London! I prefer my nomads any day.'

'So do the Thesigers, Geoff. It's one of the reasons they become adventurers.'

'I suppose being a novelist has something to do with this? I mean, this glee of yours over metropolitan skul-duggery. After all, it's all there in that *Ticklebeast* thing of yours, isn't it? A latter-day English Balzac, I said to myself when I read it.'

'Oh no you didn't!'

'Oh yes I did. He thinks he's Balzac reincarnate, I said to myself. You've begun to look a bit like Balzac actually, do you know that?'

'No I haven't, not by any stretch… But you may well be right, Geoff. I hadn't thought of any of that. It simply hadn't occurred to me.'

'Oh yes it had. Devious old sod.'

Companionably, they finished their sandwiches and drained the bottle between them. Hayward sloped off eventually to his matinee. There was so little of him, Sam thought. His rumpled old suit looked virtually empty, as though it walked itself about. A real nomad of a suit, if ever there were one.

Hearteningly tickled, Sam drove home to Kew and put in an immediate telephone call to Julian Rosenberg, who was not at home.

*

Sam pottered: did the garden and mowed the lawn; went shopping in Richmond and laid in food and drink on the assumption that his son, Joe, would drift in unannounced but expecting to be fed; made beds; tidied things up a bit; got his French notes for the new novel into some sort of not very convincing shape on the word processor.

He knew that as yet his idea lacked the energy it needed to generate shape and structure. Since the prizewinning *Ticklebeast*, with its Balzacian glee in the self-seeking machinations of the denizens of the high-rise, plate-glass megaliths of the City, a kind of ultra-contemporary, Jacobean black comedy, as one critic had acutely and enthusiastically categorised it, Sam had coasted perhaps a little too easily on the strength of plaudits and commissions for documentary films, which had taken him to a number of places he had long wished to know at first hand. But now the novel nagged at him, because the novel for Sam was essentially what writing was about. How effortlessly Hayward had pinpointed the lineage of his success of three years previously! It was for such people, after all, that Sam wrote; and somewhere within him a renewal of purpose stirred. Meanwhile he pondered the matter of the travel feature. Mary Kingsley was an attractive proposition. Sam adored independent women, could not abide the other kind. But then, Kinglake would make for an equally entertaining piece. Although it might look as though Africa, one way or another, were becoming too much of a focus, with Saggers as well. A variety of two or three possible scenarios would seem to be the answer for the moment. Then he would await developments from Hopley. From Hopley's end. Any developments your end? He lapsed back easily into the idiom of *Ticklebeast* in which he had contrived, to some comic effect, to parody a certain mode of speech. The speech of Saggers, he realised. Only there had been no irony in Saggers. Not a trace.

Late one afternoon Julian Rosenberg telephoned.

'Sam? Julian Rosenberg. You wanted words?'

'I did. I thought you should know that when I got to Hopley's preliminary do the other day Saggers was there, as one of the writing team.'

'Was he now? This is interesting. Who else?'

'The other writers? Geoff Hayward—'

'Is that *Following the Reindeer* Hayward?'

'It is. And Nigel Wheatley. *Notes From the Back of Beyond.*'

'Right. Anyone else?'

'Only me. For the moment. There were originally to be six of us, though.'

'Other names?'

'No.'

'I see. Yes, I think I do.'

'That's more than I do. Hayward was fairly obscene about it afterwards, actually. I can't say I was hugely pleased, either.'

'Oh, come on, Sam. It is pretty obvious after all. Hopley's no fool! He takes it into his head, or someone does—'

'Quentin Rodgers.'

'What's he got to do with it?'

'He's producing the series.'

'Is he? Having danced attendance on one of my daughters for most of last year... Anyway, they know who the writers are to do the kind of thing they've got in mind, but the thing is that their first three look, well, just a bit sort of... pink, as it were, so to speak. If you see what I mean. So friend Hopley buys in a spot of pinstripe stoogery to stiffen up the look of it all. That's what.'

'Right. Presumably old Sir Nicholas hopefully-to-be is under surveillance himself, from the noisome shadows of wherever?'

'You can count on that, my boy. However, where Saggers is concerned, "buy" is the operative word. I think I'm going to ask for rather more money for you than I had in mind. Good, Sam. Just remind me, will you, what that fiction prize was you won, and with what and when?'

'Courier, 1989. With a novel called *Ticklebeast*. Sort of... about the City.'

'Right. I remember. The characters all talked the way you do—'

'Not strictly all, Julian. And listen, don't forget Geoff and Nigel, will you? I know you're not acting for them, but Geoff's reindeer book won a prize too and Nigel's has done rather well. Very well, in fact. He was telling me. They're both quality men in their own right. I'll swear Hayward's still wearing the suit he had at Cambridge, though.'

'Do you imagine it went to Lappland with him too? And what's the other guy like?'

'Much younger than everybody else, but very good. He's still an academic for the moment, I think. Joe should be able to tell me when he turns up. But a confident, good-humoured, bright-looking character. Hugely amused by it all and very sure of himself. Very positive body language, as they say.'

'Pity there wasn't a cartoonist on hand – you must have looked quite a bunch. Anyway, look, Sam, I'll get onto it, right?'

'Right. Cheers, Julian.'

'Be in touch.'

His own man again, Sam grilled lamb chops and kidneys, made a green salad with some of his precious French groundnut oil, unpacked a Reblochon cheese, decanted himself a generous jugful of red *vin de table*. Afterwards, a further, long look at *Eminent Adventurers* would be in order; Lytton, whatever else he had been, was a writer whose suggestive abilities were not in question. To Sam there was, with him, the sense of a world that was altogether larger and more complex beyond, or perhaps even framing the particular limits of his narrative. Lytton, in the most down-to-earth way, was a thought-provoking writer, a writer's writer whose texts themselves could prove the tools of a trade.

In the mellow light of his reading lamp, Sam leafed through the book, with its faint odour of dust and its yellowing pages. The typeface was not one he recognised, but something which must have gone out of fashion since Lytton's day. Probably, though, you would be able to find it among the fonts of some software package, if you were minded to do so. Sam browsed, sipped at strong Italian coffee.

…there is, however, an important sense in which our best lady adventurers have much more to offer in the way of that disinterested, independent-minded disposition to set out motivated by sheer curiosity than

is the case with the empire-builders, fortune-seekers
and fugitives who people the predominantly male
precincts of the literature of travel. One cannot but
marvel at the exploits of such as Lady Mary Wortley
Montagu, Amelia Edwards, Mary Kingsley and others
who asserted a basic right as human beings, the right
to freedom of movement about this globe which, regrettably, is still too frequently denied to their sex not
only by heathen and exotic cultures but also, shame-
fully, by the conventions of our very own. The great
ages to which they lived, many of these ladies, the
brilliant eccentricities which characterised them, the
fine works of travel literature they left as testimony to
lives lived on a larger scale than the vast majority, all
make their contribution to an assertion of funda-
mental truth where the fact of human sexuality is in
question that most cultures, benighted as indeed they
are for whatever reasons, so obtusely deny...

Sam was intrigued. He had quite forgotten this part of
Lytton's introduction. Clearly, there had been a great deal
more to him than the waspish, homosexual, iconoclast
aspect of his character might have led a reader to believe. A
complex fellow. Sam read on.

...it is a fortunate quirk of historical fact that so few
of these intrepid ladies did actually meet with the
kind of untoward end they so frequently and enthusiastically appear, many of them, to have avoided
by a hair's breadth or even less, if of course they are
to be believed entirely in their tale-telling. Indeed,
the only case I can recall or have been able to trace of
unmitigated and even, most probably, tragic disaster
where such an English lady was involved has been
that of Miss Eleanor Tew, whose disappearance in

the early 1880s somewhere in the Bakhtiari Mountains of south-western Persia has simply never been satisfactorily accounted for. It goes, I should aver, without saying that a cultivated lady such as Miss Tew, as an erstwhile member of an early generation of Cambridge ladies must surely have been, would without doubt have kept a journal of her experiences, especially given the reputation she had already established for herself as a writer with her books on Bavaria and the Pyrenees, both of which had been published in the '70s of last century in the popular 'Books for Travellers' series by Messrs Chatto & Windus. Now, clearly, the Bakhtiari Mountains must amount to a very different proposition from the Bavarian highlands and even the Pic du Midi de Bigorre or the Cirque de Gavarnie. So we are led to wonder, did the ill-fated expedition in question represent an attempt on the part of this lady from Leamington Spa to establish herself amongst those great and intrepid ladies of exploration and adventure of the kind I have already mentioned? Or does my question, thus worded, impart a false notion of motive? Regrettably, these are questions it is impossible to answer. It seems therefore that the disappearance of Eleanor Tew is likely to remain one of the unsolved mysteries of exploration.

Sam was intrigued. Eleanor Tew of Leamington Spa was not a name that featured in the annals of travel as far as he knew. He was also taken by the way in which Lytton had qualified his own rather facile immediate assumption that the Bakhtiari expedition had been a bid for greater consequence on the part of Miss Tew. 'Does my question, thus worded, impart a false notion of motive?' Certainly, Sam's own writer's instinct would suspect the matter to have been otherwise and more complex. A Cambridge lady in 1870 whenever... for such it appeared she had been. Surely one of almost the first generation of Miss Clough's protégées. Somewhere there a story lay waiting: he recognised this with a lift of the heart. For such a person would simply never 'aspire to establish herself among the ranks of...' or whatever it was. Such people tended very definitely to be their own man. Or woman. So what could have become of this Victorian lady explorer? Had her life been curtailed in some remote spot by a matter of mundane accident? Or what? The more he pondered the question the more imponderables he found. Presumably, for instance, she must have been searched for: the Foreign Office must have been involved. Sam was prepared to wager that Eleanor Tew of Leamington Spa had come of a family that would have been not only influential but informed and worldly-wise. They would have possessed both the resources and the know-how to initiate extensive enquiries in the appropriate quarters, whether at home or in Tehran. What could possibly have transpired in consequence?

Sam thought he would look out for the Bavarian book and particularly, in view of his own interest in that part of France, the Pyrenean book. Meanwhile his contribution to Hopley's project was a matter of more pressing concern.

The doorbell rang, a thunderously insistent, unnecessarily continuous, familiar, deliberately intrusive sort of ring. On the doorstep stood the most enormous young man in denim, bearded and bronzed, with a huge rucksack on one shoulder and beside him, on his other side, an elegant little girl with short raven-black hair stylishly cut and wearing what looked to Sam like a blouse of Florentine silk, flamboyant and un-English and daringly coloured.

'Hi, Dad,' said the giant. 'This is Emma. May we come in?'

'Yes, Joe. Do,' he said. 'Hello, Emma.'

'Hello, Mr Webster.'

They shook hands and the girl smiled up at him. A smile to stop a strong man in his tracks, Sam thought.

'Emma?'

'Emma Rosenberg, Dad.'

So this was Julian's daughter. Or one of them.

'Emma just fetched me from Victoria, Dad. I've been roaming the Mani for a bit, looking at some of the places that old mate of yours wrote about ages ago. I could have looked him up, but I didn't.'

'Paddy Leigh Fermor.'

'That's the one. Anyway, we had an Italian in Putney, and Emma's just dropping me off, if that's all right.'

'Of course it's all right. Do come in, my dear.'

'Ooh, I say! Is that a malt?'

'It is. Help yourself, Joe. And you, Emma.'

'No, thank you, Mr Webster. I've got to drive back to Hampstead after this and we've already had some wine. But… is that Italian coffee I can smell?'

'Lavazza d'Oro, if it's all the same to you.'

'Ooh, yes please. How delicious.'

'But positively nothing boozy to go with it?'

'Absolutely not, thanks all the same. I say, Joe?'

'Yes, darling?'

'You sort of… Well, not to put too fine a point on it, you pong a bit, d'you realise?'

'Do I offend your delicate metropolitan sensibilities then, sweetikin? Of course I pong. I've tramped across half Greece, haven't I? And kipped on deck up the Adriatic and been on a train for the best part of a week.'

'Okay, sorry. I mean, I don't mind a bit, but it's, well, not sort of generally pleasant for everyone, is it?'

'Okay, Em. I'll be having a bath later, I promise. And I'll deal with you tomorrow.'

'Yes, please.'

Returning with the coffee, Sam caught just the last of this exchange. The beginning of an affair? How enviably unself-conscious and easy it could be, when the match was a good one. Having now spent weeks on his own, Sam warmed to the idea of having Joe in the house for a while, with all that would entail of friends, this girl, the comings and goings, the telephone calls, the plans and projects.

'Mr Webster, I gather my father's handling some television work for you at the moment? Not that I make a habit of quizzing him over his authors, please don't think that. Or that he would tell me if I did, for that matter.'

'You're quite right, he is.'

'What's this then, Dad?'

'A series on travellers, Joe. I'm writing one of the programmes for Nick Hopley.'

'Right. Nige's in on this, too, isn't he?'

'Nige? You mean Nigel Wheatley? I didn't know you knew him.'

'Sure. Research Fellow at Cath's in my final year. Terrific company.'

'You mean you got drunk with him. He means he got drunk with him.'

'God, women! Yes, I suppose you could put it like that.'

'Crudely, you mean?'

'I do, yes. But yes, I did. Lots. So there. In fact, Dad...'

'Yes?'

'It will be all right to stay for a bit, won't it?'

'Of course. I was expecting you to.'

'I mean, I thought I'd rather like to see old Nige again, and one or two of the others, so perhaps we could have a barbecue or something eventually and you could meet him properly, on a social basis rather than just a work one.'

'Nice idea, Joe.'

'Well, you know. Given that the weather seems to be holding up very nicely here this summer. I was dreading being cold here, actually. It's always the same when you come back up from the Mediterranean, I think.'

'I know what you mean. I only drove back from the cottage a couple of weeks ago.'

'Where's that, Mr Webster?'

'In the Pyrenees not far from Pau.'

'So, Dad. A barbecue? Just a few of us.'

'Including me.'

'Yes, Emma. Including you.'

'And we could find you a bird, Dad. If you want.'

'Ant. Or Just?'

'Exactly. Either, really.'

'Perfect. Brilliant!'

They were looking into one another's eyes and laughing, her eyes all aglint with intelligence and mischief. Intrigued as he was by what he discerned of some tacit, coded thing between them, Sam demurred.

'Thank you, but I'm perfectly capable of providing for myself...'

And in response to Joe's raised eyebrow.

'Maria most likely, I should think.'

'Maria Brooke? Oh yes, definitely.'

'Maria Brooke? Really? Oh do, Mr Webster. I've never met her, and her last collection of short stories was absolutely fabulous. Everyone at Clough read them. Everyone!'

'She'll be delighted to hear that. That's her old college too, you know.'

'No, I didn't.'

'I used to play tennis against her for Queens'. We had a gentleman's fixture in Sidgwick Avenue.'

'Gosh! I say, it does sort of, well, stick with you, all that, doesn't it?'

'It does, yes. With most people, I imagine. Are you going to miss it, d'you think, Emma?'

He had remembered from something Julian had told him that this daughter had recently completed a modern languages degree.

'I am actually, yes. More than I thought I would, I mean, with London and all the rest of it. I've always adored our London life, and the continent and things. I lived in Munich and Sienna for a bit and we've had our house in Provence for as long as I can remember... But I shall miss it, yes.'

'It stays with you, my dear. Through your friends and through what you brought away with you in terms of an attitude of mind, a... style, if you like. When you walked in with Joe just now, you were instantly recognisable for what you are. The rest is mere nostalgia, a potent nostalgia of course, but a sentimental self-indulgence nevertheless—'

'Such as the moral tradition most urgently enjoins us to eschew? In this univarsitah.'

'It does, I suppose actually, yes. Because the real essence of the Cambridge thing is dispassionate and Greek and anti-sentimentality, or so I like to think. It probably isn't anything like entirely true, given the abundance of prats everywhere, but it's a part of my idealised view. A private sentimentality if you like. Now there's a nice irony for you.'

'I say, Mr Webster?'

'Yes?'

'Joe's asleep.'

'So he is. He ought to go to bed, I suppose. How did he get back, do you know? He can't have trained it through Yugoslavia, or whatever it calls itself these days, can he?'

'No, no. He got some appalling, smelly old boat up the Adriatic to Venice apparently and came on from there by train. But I'd better be going, much as I'd love to stay and talk to you, Mr Webster. Joe!'

'I wasn't asleep.'

'Oh, yes you were. Anyway, I'm going.'

Gargantuan stirrings ensued from the depths of the arm-chair into which Joe had subsided. Sam saw them to the door.

'We shall meet again, I hope.'

'So do I, Mr Webster. It's been really nice talking to you.'

He left them there and turned back into the house. A few moments later a car outside started up and drove away.

★

Voices filled the garden as young people drifted in and out of the house through the French windows. There was the meaty fragrance of a barbecue on the drifting smoke. Sam eyed his trolley of bottles, uncorked another red and watched Joe watching Emma mix a dressing for a green salad.

'Might be a bit sharp, this. It's how I like it, but what do you think?'

'Terrific! Absolutely *al dente.*'

'*Allora, va bene così.*'

Impeccable utterance. Cambridge modern languages with a touch of Jewish histrionics, intimations of the South in a green English garden.

'Hi.'

Maria slipped an arm about his waist, kissed him companionably on the cheek.

'Hello, darling. How're you doing?'

'Absolutely fine. Aren't they all nice? Where d'you get them?'

'Joe's, mainly. Nigel's doing a programme in the series. Have you read his book?'

'Gorgeous! An absolute hoot. I mean, honestly, *Notes From the Back of Beyond*! But that is exactly what it is.'

'You're held in some regard here yourself, you know. Apparently, you have a fair old Clough following.'

'Really? How d'you know that?'

'Emma.'

'The little dark one with Joe, with the enviably gorgeous frontage? Who is she?'

'Julian's daughter. One of Julian's daughters. He's got dozens, as far as I can make out. Not that that's got anything to do with it. But she did say that "the whole college" had read your last collection of short stories.'

'*Whirligig*? How nice! I must speak to her. And who is Antonia?'

'Now that I do not know. Except that they threatened me with either Ant or Just and Just hasn't made it so this is Ant. She's one of the Oxford ones. In publishing and lives in Greenwich.'

'Doesn't it take you back?'

'It certainly does. They're better with each other, though, than we were. We must have been pretty chronic, one way and another.'

'Parents had more sway in our day. And the values of their generation. These kids have a much more definite sense of a culture of their own.'

'You could be right. But we have contrived to make up for some things.'

'We sure have. Sam?'

'Yes?'

'You wouldn't like to spend the late autumn in Provence with me, would you? I've got this place I bought near Nîmes, and I'm off in a week or two to get in what's left of the summer and then to work on a new novel. Why don't you drop in for a bit? I could use some unobtrusive company, someone to talk to when I'm not writing.'

'It's a marvellous thought, Maria, thank you. Although I simply must write this television thing first for Hopley.

118

Perhaps in October? I have only just come back from the Pyrenees.'

'Whenever you like, Sam. Just let me know. Rue du Cadran Solaire, Pic Saint Loup.'

'Maria?'

'Yes?'

'Have you ever come across the name Eleanor Tew?'

'Eleanor Tew? No, I don't think I have. Why?'

'Oh, a reference that rather intrigued me. Charles Lytton, *Eminent Adventurers*.'

'Yes?'

'He mentions her in his introduction as an example of the lady explorer who never was. He says: "the only case I can recall of unmitigated disaster where an English lady traveller was involved was that of Eleanor Tew, whose disappearance has never been satisfactorily accounted for". Or more or less, anyway.'

'And where did she disappear?'

'South-west Persia. The Bakhtiari Mountains.'

'Hmm, no. Sorry. Can't help.'

'Dad!'

'Yes, Joe?'

'The meat's done; this first lot anyway. We can make a start, everyone.'

'Mr Webster?'

'My dear?'

'I'm Antonia James. I don't know if you got my name before, but I overheard what you were just telling your friend. I can tell you a bit about Eleanor Tew.'

A tall, slender girl. Long blonde hair and, unusually, brown eyes.

'Good lord! Can you really?'

'Well, it's a bit complicated in fact, and I don't know all that much, but—'

'Never mind. You just tell me what you do know. Come over here a minute.'

Sam appropriated a bottle, refilled their glasses and sat the girl down in a corner away from the noise.

'Now.'

'Right. When we, that is my family, lived in Warwickshire and I went to school there, I had a best friend called Virginia Barraclough, whose mother had a great-great-aunt I think it was, called Anna Rowlandson. Mrs B was named after her, as a matter of fact. Anyway, Anna Rowlandson was Eleanor Tew's close friend and travelling companion on the trip described in Miss Tew's *Bavarian Journal*. Mrs Barraclough had a copy of that because Anna Rowlandson had been the illustrator. She drew the plants and the flowers, the rocks and forests, lakes and mountains – lovely sketches. You could write to her in Warwick, couldn't you? The Tudor House, High Street, Warwick. Mrs Reginald Barraclough. Her husband's a local GP.'

'Antonia, I'm overwhelmed. Really and truly. I just don't know what to say to you.'

'You could say, 'Have another glass of this marvellous claret.'

'I'm sorry. Darling girl, have the whole bottle.'

'So, may one ask why you are interested in Eleanor Tew?'

'There's a reference in Charles Lytton's *Eminent Adventurers* to her having disappeared without trace—'

'That's right. No one ever did learn what became of her, actually. You would have thought that her father would have been capable of tracing her somehow or other, after all. He was a man of standing and influence in Warwickshire at the time—'

'Do you know what sort of man?'

'He was an independent gentleman first and foremost, but he was also the borough engineer of Leamington Spa.'

'Was he indeed?'

'Which is why I maintain that he, of all people, should have able to put in hand the kind of investigation, through the Foreign Office for instance, which might have cast crucial light upon his daughter's disappearance. Unless…'

'Unless what?'

'Unless of course, she, for whatever reason, engineered the disappearance to make it impossible for anyone to find out the facts of the matter.'

'I suppose that is a possibility. For whatever reason.'

'For whatever reason. I mean, I just don't know. But certainly no one ever did learn what became of her, that's for sure.'

'This gets more and more interesting. I was hugely intrigued in the first place, but now… I'm supposed to be writing a piece on… probably Mary Kingsley for a TV series, which is why I just happened to be browsing through Lytton.'

'This is the thing Nigel's doing Fawcett for, isn't it?'

'That's right.'

'Nigel's obsessed with Fawcett. For the moment. Momentary obsessions are rather his thing.'

'Well, there you are. I think, you know, I'm getting more interested in Eleanor Tew than I am in Mary Kingsley, though I must finish this job first before I even consider starting something completely new. Because there could be a story in all this somewhere. I shall write to your friend's mother, so thank you very much.'

'And you'll let me know what transpires, won't you? I shall be positively agog to learn what you find out.'

'Well, that's the fun of it all really, isn't it? How about a chop or two and a mouthful of salad to go with that claret?'

'Good idea. I must say, I am rather hungry.'

Dear Mr Webster,

I was greatly interested by your letter concerning Miss
Tew and my great-great-aunt, Anna Rowlandson, whose
Christian name I bear, as you will see from my signature. I
suppose this is the way research is done; I have to confess that
I had not considered the matter in any detail before.

It was nice, too, to have news of Antonia. I suppose it
must be the best part of ten years now since she and our
daughter Virginia were best friends in the sixth form at the
King's High School here in Warwick. As Antonia lived out
in the country on the far side of Leamington Spa, she would
often stay the night with us after a theatre trip to Stratford or
a party or whatever, and then what crashings and bangings,
what shrieks of laughter from the kitchen into the small
hours! Gin and Tonic my husband used to call them, and so
they were!

I can tell you quite a bit about Eleanor Tew and the Tew
family of Leamington Spa. We possess, among our books, a
first edition of the Bavarian Journal which my great-great-
aunt illustrated. Unfortunately, we do not have the
Pyrenean Excursion. Perhaps you can enquire at Hay-on-
Wye or get a book-search concern to find it for you.

My husband and I should be delighted to see you for
lunch or tea if you felt it worth your while to make the trip
up here one day. It is really not all that far nowadays, with
the new M40, and our house, in the very centre of Warwick,
is easily identified, right opposite the Lord Leycester Hospital
by the gate tower which leads to the Stratford road.

Perhaps you might let us know in advance if and when
you propose to take me up on this. There is one other thing.
We wonder if you would be good enough to autograph our
copies of your novels? My husband has a fair collection of

122

hard-back first editions of contemporary novelists, and, since
we are both great admirers, yours are all there.

Yours sincerely,
Anna Barraclough

Chapter Three

The Tudor House was precisely what its name so flatly stated; it squatted, in picturesque, defiant angularity, on the very crest of the gradient of the High Street, at the point where the road plunged sharply downwards round the old gate tower in the direction of Stratford-upon-Avon.

Inside there was not a floor which was level or a door cut as a true rectangle, but the homely, unpretentious character of the Barracloughs and the things that furnished and embellished the house provided a reassuring contrast to the zanier, Lewis Carroll aspects of the dwelling. After lunch they sat over coffee in a cosy, chintzy den overlooking the street, across which, perfectly framed in the Barracloughs' window, stood the half-timbered, medieval almshouses of the great Lord of Leycester. It was a sight of unspeakable, unforgettable magnificence.

'At night-time, Mr Webster, the façade's floodlit. Can you imagine? We very rarely draw the curtains in here. Fortunately, we don't get too many passers-by at this end of the street. So we have our own *lumière*, you see, without the *son*.'

Reginald Barraclough was a genial, bald-headed character with twinkling, good-humoured brown eyes.

'But I'm going to leave you to Anna now, Mr Webster, as medicine calls. Do sign your books, won't you?'

'I'll do them immediately, doctor, before it slips my mind. And thank you for your hospitality.'

'Our pleasure, my dear fellow.'

'Back sooner or later?'

'Yes, darling. Back sooner or later.'

A familiar-looking pile of volumes was placed on the coffee table beside Sam. 'Good heavens! You've even got *Up at a Villa*! My first! It never sold at all well, you know. In fact, I thought I'd had it as a novelist after that, so I never did write *Down in the City* and I certainly never shall now. How hideously Italianistic it all was!'

'Yes, I suppose you could say that about it, although in fact that was rather what we, well, liked about it, you know. Both of us. Independently.'

'How extraordinary! You know, Mrs Barraclough, you never can anticipate let alone calculate the effect of a novel on readers.'

'How very disconcerting! So what do you do?'

'Be as interesting as you know how to be and hope for the best, I suppose.'

'And isn't that somewhat... hit or miss?'

'Very hit or miss. One ends up doing it simply because one enjoys it, I suppose.'

'That must be true of a lot of things, I imagine.'

'Certainly it is. Anyway, do tell me about your great-great-aunt, if you would. I can go through these as I listen to you.'

'Would you just have a look at this first, please?'

Anna Barraclough picked a volume from the table beside her and handed it to him, open at the flyleaf, where there was an inscription. It read: 'To my dearest Anna, in memory of that splendid time, this, a special copy in love and esteem from your Eleanor'.

Faded ink, a gracious, cursive Victorian script. Sam found himself looking at the handwriting of Eleanor Tew; he was conscious of a strong urge to shed tears as a casual reference, almost a footnote even, suddenly became the once living reality of a unique individual. The fact of an untimely disappearance, of what must surely have been a brilliant, exceptional life rudely curtailed, made the thing all the more poignant. He spoke with some difficulty, in awareness of the damnable tragic enigma with which he had chosen to engage and which was beginning to exert a compulsion all of its own upon his sympathies.

'I don't know what to say', he managed eventually.

'I did that on purpose, you know.'

The tone of voice was composed, exploring, very sure of itself.

'I know you did.'

'So now I know you are nice and genuine, literally *bona fide*, in fact.' Anna Barraclough pronounced the Latin correctly, giving the long 'a' of the adjective its proper value. 'You see, Mr Webster, I simply couldn't just have let you in on things concerning my family now, could I? I mean, if you'd just been journalistically curious or something. It would not have done.'

'I never thought. I'm so sorry. One gets so intent on finding out... It's a kind of curiosity one cultivates, on the lookout for stories.'

'I'm beginning to appreciate that. And also how one takes it for granted that stories, well, just sort of happen.'

'Believe me, Mrs Barraclough, they do not. Not by any means.'

'Anyway...'

'Yes?'

'At the time of the disappearance of Eleanor Tew in 1882 – that's right, isn't it?'

'According to Lytton, yes.'

'Ah yes. Charles Lytton. Horrible little man. By 1882 my great-great-aunt Anna had entered the teaching profession. Within a very few years she had become a headmistress – at a time, as I'm sure you know, when the education of girls of the middle classes was beginning to gather strength

largely in consequence of what had been achieved by Miss
Davies and Miss Clough in Cambridge and, of course, by
others elsewhere, with protégées like my great-great-aunt
and Miss Tew in the early instances. But she soon abandoned her career in education to marry, at a rather
advanced age according to the expectations of the day, a
clergyman, Jonathan Hebblethwaite, then died giving birth
to her first child, a son, George, named in accordance with
her wish after her brother George, who had been killed in
action against the Zulu at Isandhlwana, at the same time as
his great friend and companion, one imagines, in high
cockalorum, Captain William Tew.'

'William Tew?'

'A brother. There were six Tews, Mr Webster. Twin
boys, both army officers, then Eleanor, then three more
girls called, if I remember rightly, Rachel, Gwendolen and
Jemima in that order. But, anyway, George Hebblethwaite
was my great-uncle, his wife's sister being my grand-
mother. Technically, you see, Anna Rowlandson was not
quite an aunt, I don't think, though that is how we've
always thought of her. All right so far?'

'Terrific. But what about the father?'

'My dear sir, Theophilus Tew must be worth a least a
tome in his own right. I'll get onto him, if I may, in due
course. But first, Eleanor Tew…'

It was much later than he had anticipated when Sam
eventually took his leave of the Barracloughs.

'You've been absolutely marvellous. Really and truly, I
couldn't have hoped for more, and I am indescribably
grateful.'

'And what will you do now, my dear fellow?'

'I don't know, you know. For the moment, anyway. The
obvious thing would be to turn one's attention to the
disappearance, don't you think? Although I'm sure I have

no idea how one might do that, since no one seems to know anything about it.'

'There might be just one possibility, you know. Can't think why I didn't think of it earlier, but why don't you try Clough Hall? There might be something there, don't you think, in the archives or whatever they have? They store away all kinds of old junk, don't they, these places? From what I've heard, anyway. And you just never know, do you? So what have you got to lose by asking?'

'Doctor Barraclough, you're a genius! I suppose it should have been obvious, although these things never do seem to be, somehow. I'll let you know what transpires, shall I?'

'Do, my dear fellow. And next time you come up, you just bring your tennis things and we'll have a game at the Boat Club. We drink pints in the showers there, you know. It's a tradition.'

'I'll look forward to that.'

Chapter Four

Sam returned to London and made various contacts, then wrote to the Principal at Clough and worked on the Kingsley project for Nick Hopley.

'I say, Sam,' said Nigel Wheatley one evening, on a brief visit with Joe, 'can you see Saggers doing the Bedouin? I mean, the mind positively boggles at the thought, does it not? I know mine does. But he'll have to, won't he? Because if you want to do nomads you've got to live the nomad life, I should have thought. I can't see that happening, I really can't.'

'Like Geoff Hayward with his Lapps? No, I can't say I can either. Besides, he must be too busy with his other interests, I should think. Strange thing for Nick to do, though, really. Not like him at all.'

'Television does seem to be in a bit of a state, one way or another, at this moment in time, wouldn't you say? They all seem to be terrified and anticipating all sorts of repercussions most of the time.'

'I'm not surprised. Are you? But you're right – it's all got extremely nasty, and the sort of people Saggers is identified with are largely responsible.'

'Bit hard to take, isn't it?'

'That reminds me, Dad,' Joe joined in from the depths of an armchair, 'Emma wrote to say she'd watched a fantastic documentary on French TV on Thesiger. *The White Bédouin. Le Bédouin Blanc.* She said to tell you.'

'Now there's an interesting thought!'

'Indeed.'

'Sam?'

'Yes, Nigel?'

'Do you imagine brother Hopley knows his friend's thing has already been done on French television? Because I really think he should, don't you?'

'You nasty young man. I can see you're going to go a very long way.'

'He's going to end up in your mate's sort of job. Hopsack, or whatever he's called.'

'Balls, Joe!'

'Oh yes, you will.'

'Then I'll be the only M'bhutu-speaking zec in telly.'

'Don't you count on it, laddie. They come ten a penny, men like you. Speaking in strange tongues an' all that—'

'Codses. Anyway, I'm off. Thanks for the drinks, Sam. And don't let him have any more of that malt.'

'I'll bear it in mind. How's Fawcett, by the way?'

'Oh, brilliant. There's a whole lot of stuff, actually. Then there's Peter Fleming, you know. I'm not quite sure whether I'm doing Fawcett or Fleming at the moment but it will resolve itself in due course, as these things tend to do. And Kingsley? Or is it Kinglake?'

'Kingsley. Lots of fun. A very... bubbly lady. Died aged thirty-eight, of something she must have caught nursing Boer prisoners of war in South Africa. I seem to be into early death at the moment, one way or another.'

'Do you? How's that?'

'Oh, just something else I've vaguely got on for the future. Anyway, listen, Nigel. Leave Hopley to me, won't you? He is an old mate of mine – oh yes, from university days. We used to write things together for Footlights. I'll make a point of seeing him as soon as I can. We meet for lunch, now and again. That's actually how all this came up, after my Channel Four thing on Provençal shepherds.'

'I remember that. In fact, I've got it in my tape collection. Great stuff. Oh, and I'll tell Ant what you said about the Barracloughs.'

'And pass on oriental gratitudes.'

'Indeed, indeed. I think I met Virginia Barraclough once, you know. A gorgeous, bosomy little bird with red hair and a pretty sharp tongue, a real Titian. Ant's a Florentine, of course, a sort of reincarnation of Simonetta Vespucci, from the Botticellis in the Uffizi. Anyway, chiz. Joe, write from Munich, won't you?'

'Surely. Can you never get out of a house?'

'Okay, okay, this very minute.'

And Nigel went.

Chapter Five

Clough in January, Cambridge in January, was as cold as Sam remembered it from thirty years previously. In Sidgwick Avenue the trees, invariably pictured in the memory as a paradisal summer riot of blossom and foliage against the warm red brick of the main college buildings, were stark and bare, crazily skeletal in their petrified dance up the avenue as far as Grange Road.

Turning into the main entrance of the college, Sam recollected a snatch of Granados, from the *Allegro de Concierto*, demisemiquaver triplets played in masterly style on a piano somewhere up in Selwyn across the road, unmistakably Spanish harmonies drifting down through the balmy loveliness of a May evening as he had strolled by with an adored companion whose identity had now completely slipped his mind. Was this what was in store for Joe and Emma, Nigel and Antonia? But, he told himself with some impatience, the power to haunt was merely one of the more inconvenient side effects of memory's function. One was too inclined to ascribe undue meaning to past experience – it was the way of the mind. But, try as he might, Sam could not recall the name of the girl who had shared that moment with him. And that was the fact of the matter.

He was given coffee by the Senior Tutor, a brisk, iron-grey, capable lady, in a panelled sitting room overlooking the gardens where Sam had used to play tennis, eat strawberries and flirt.

'Naturally, we do possess all manner of material pertaining to the lives of quondam members. Miss Tew, of course, was virtually as far back as the college goes. There may be things, though I'm not aware that there are, but I'm going to pass you on to the librarian, or at least to her assistant since she herself is away at present, and you may quiz her to your heart's content, Mr Webster. I'm quite sure she will be delighted to entertain you.'

Sam decided to ignore that; he would get his own back sooner or later.

'I'm most grateful, Senior Tutor. Thank you.'

'I think I should warn you, though, Mr Webster, that I hold it unlikely there is anything of great interest amongst our possessions. I understand that the lady in question met with an untimely end at a relatively early age without having attained distinction either remarkable or acknowledged. Had she made a name for herself in scholarship or philanthropy perhaps... No, almost certainly there would have been something. But as a mere one of the many worthy former members whose lives, for all their individual value, are led in unremarkable obscurity... Do you take my point, sir?'

'I do, madam. Your point is plain enough.'

'However, you shall speak with Miss Rainsford, who is expecting you.'

*

Doctor Jacquetta Rainsford, the youngest fellow of the college, proved to be as young and bubbly as the Senior Tutor was iron and determinedly middle-aged. She was delighted to meet Sam, with whose novels she was appreciatively familiar, intrigued by the thought of Eleanor Tew, about whom she had known nothing, and eager to be told more as well as to probe the nature of Sam's interest in her case. By profession a historian, she had something of the novelist's fascination with the minutiae of human behaviour and, exceptionally for her kind it seemed to Sam, with its quirks and oddities. And, despite her sporadic attempts at scholarly gravitas, Jacquetta Rainsford frothed and chattered. Sam pictured her in a tea shop, and thought he might quite like to be there with her.

'There's nothing on the computer, I'm afraid. I've already been through the lot. Which doesn't of course mean there's nothing in existence, only that it's not on disk, whatever it may be.'

'What exactly were you told I wanted?'

'I was told that you were a writer, a novelist of some apparent reputation – which I knew already anyway, only the Senior Tutor quite obviously didn't – who was interested in a former member, one Eleanor Tew, who was one of an early generation of Miss Clough's ladies here and who had died a premature and untimely death about which nothing was known, it having occurred in some remote part of the world.'

'Why "untimely", if the manner of it is not known?'

'I wondered about that. But I'm merely repeating verbatim what I was told.'

'Verbatim?'

'Absolutely. There was a question mark, wasn't there?'

'Oh, I don't doubt you. But perhaps there was just the suggestion of one, I have to allow. I don't often meet with such precision.'

'I'm sorry if that was a bit aggressive. You see, there are those, that woman for one, who think I'm a fribble. It has to do with my manner and the way I look. But I'm not. I know more about ante-Revolution aristocratic French ladies than almost anyone in the world.'

'I believe you.'

'Oh, I knew you would. I've read you, don't forget.'

'So you have. So that's your particular interest, Miss Rainsford, is it?'

'My fellowship dissertation was on the political influence of royal mistresses at the court of Louis XIV, which does actually cause some people to imagine that I aspire to the condition of Nancy Mitford, or something equally ludicrous. The supposition I mean, not Miss Mitford.'

'Yes, I do see. I don't imagine novelists are particularly *gratae* in those quarters, either.'

'Correct. But the Principal was behind you.'

'True. Thanks to a wicked London connection. Well, perhaps not quite wicked, exactly.' Sam could not resist something of a snort of amusement.

'May one ask who?'

'The Archbishop of York. I used to play squash with him at Queens'. And she was his girlfriend. Your Principal, I mean.'

'Bloody hell!' said Jacquetta Rainsford. 'How utterly delicious! May I dine out on that? At least, among my friends. Look, why don't we just search the stack a bit? I mean, you just never know, do you?'

'No, you don't.'

'In fact, that's rather the thing about any kind of research, don't you agree?'

'I do actually, yes.'

'I remember the most extraordinary coincidence when I read a fantastic novel by Peter Levi. I was in the sixth form then, and, anyway, in this novel there was a reference to the equestrian statue of the Emperor Marcus Aurelius on the Capitol Hill in Rome, which I hadn't actually seen at that time. And a couple of days later I was in the school library looking for something on Madame de Pompadour and I happened, quite idly, to pick up a rather nice-looking volume of photographs of the ancient world that was just lying on the table nearby, and it opened at – guess what?'

'The equestrian statue of the Emperor Marcus Aurelius—'

'In the Piazza del Campidoglio – precisely. It was one of the most telling moments of my life, without any doubt whatsoever. I mean, you could just scream with the delight of it, couldn't you?'

'Yes,' said Sam, 'you could.'

But the stack yielded nothing. It was the end of the search. All that remained was for Sam to take his leave.

'You've been awfully nice, to give me your time and help the way you have. Thank you,' he said.

'I haven't been much use.'

'I've enjoyed being with you. May I give you lunch?'

'No,' said Jacquetta Rainsford, 'I've got a working lunch in a college committee. But you could take me to tea and fill me up with French pâtisserie, if you're going to be here still, this afternoon. I'm particularly fond of tarte aux abricots, with lots of confectioner's custard.'

They had made their way out of the college and into the street.

'Four o'clock then, here?'

'Four fifteen, outside King's. I'll come down on my bike and save you the trouble of walking all the way back up here.'

'How very considerate. I shall be there.'

'And what will you do now, about Eleanor Tew?'

'I honestly don't know. But I am going to have a decent lunch, then stroll about Cambridge and think.'

'Something will turn up.'

'It usually does, if you go looking for it. More often than one might think likely, anyway. Look, darling, it's awfully cold. You really ought to go straight back inside.'

'Oooh!' said Jacquetta Rainsford with deliberate histrionics. 'I liked that… Sam.'

136

It was something like thirty years since the last time, but here he was again, Sam Webster, grinning inanely at a girl in Sidgwick Avenue.

★

There was a message on the answerphone from Nick Hopley when Sam eventually got back to Kew that evening. Could he ring ITE to arrange a mutually convenient time for a meeting?

Sam made himself some Italian coffee and sat himself down with a generous dram of the Edradour, or what Joe and Nigel had left of it, for sipping while he collected his thoughts.

The house was silent. After the comings and goings, the crashings and bursts of song from the bathroom, the chatter of Joe's friends, the silence pointed implacably, like the finger of doom almost, to the one sane resort of the solitary – work. Not that he would mind, since writing was what his life was about anyway, but he would miss the noise, the companionship, the fun, the easy affectionate kisses.

Eleanor Tew. It was a disappointment, after Reginald Barraclough's Clough notion had seemed such a bright idea. Momentarily, he was at a loss for what to do next, but the Kingsley project for Nick Hopley would at least keep him busy in the immediate future, and there would be other things. The notes he had made last summer in the Pyrenees still awaited his further attention. For the moment Eleanor Tew would have to wait, despite his feeling that there was very definitely something to be made of her, whether biographically or in fiction. Meanwhile he would go through his Kingsley material and telephone Nick first thing in the morning.

★

In Cambridge Jacquetta Rainsford and a friend, Nicky Vandevelde, shared a pile of beef sandwiches and a bottle of burgundy.

'This is extremely pleasant – nicer than dinner, for a change.'

'I thought we could have a bit of a natter, since I haven't seen you for so long.'

'How was Amsterdam?'

'Heaven. It really is a lovely place, you know. I just adore it. I spent a lot of time looking at paintings, actually. One never tires of them. Then there's really decent coffee and apple cake with whipped cream. What have you been up to, if one may ask? Apart from research.'

'I entertained a novelist.'

'You what! You mean, you? Or rather he? Jacques! Come on!'

'You mucky so-and-so, Nick! I did not give him my body in my official capacity as college hostess, if that's what you're hoping to hear. I mightn't have minded privately though. He was rather dishy.'

'Who was this?'

'Sam Webster.'

'The *Ticklebeast* man?' And what was he doing around these halls? That's an awfully funny book, you know. Really and truly; it has point.'

'I remember. He wanted to find out about somebody called Eleanor Tew, who apparently belonged to one of the first generations of our kind in the time of Miss Clough. Some friend had suggested to him there might be something on her amongst our college junk.'

'And was there?'

'Nothing on the computer, nothing in the stack, I'm afraid. I'd have been glad to help him because I liked him. Besides which, I could tell the Iron Duchess didn't. She hadn't a clue who he was—'

'What? She didn't know who Sam Webster was?'

'Hadn't the slightest. But he came with tremendous forces behind him. I say, Nick, you'll never guess what he told me!'

'No, I won't. Go on.'

'Well, apparently when his mate suggested he do a search at Clough he got in touch with the Archbishop of York, whom he used to play squash with when they were both at Queens', because, at that time, it appears, KH was the archbishop's girlfriend!'

'No! How utterly priceless! How did he tell it, exactly?'

'He told it as though he enjoyed telling it to me because he seemed to sense I would love it as much as he did. He was dead right.'

'He sounds rather nice, I must say. What exactly was he like?'

'Oh, tall and slender, with lovely grey hair and a mischievous, glinty-eyed face; you know.'

'Oh, wow! I say, Jacques…'

'Yes?'

'You said just now there was nothing on the computer and nothing in the stack.'

'That's right.'

'You did try the attic as well, presumably, did you?'

'What attic?'

'At Newnham Lodge. There's loads of our stuff up there, you know. It was stored for us by Corpus when we redid the library at the time the computer was installed, whenever that was. I imagine it's all still there.'

'Ow mah gawd! I'd no idea! I must tell Sam; he can come back up and we'll do another search. Nick, you're an absolute humdinger! I love you amazingly, truly and sapphonically I do!'

*

They sat round the same table as before. Hopley, Vanessa darling, Geoff Hayward, Nigel Wheatley, Sam.

'Where's the other one, then? Whatever his name was.' Hayward spoke first.

'Now, Geoff,' said Hopley, rueful, placatory, 'I have to say that I doubt if you appreciate the kind of constraints we operate under here, these days. Anyway, Saggers has pulled out. Pressure of other business, sends his apologies and regrets, sad not to be working with such an interesting and distinguished team.'

'Balls.'

'Precisely.'

'Nick, did you know there was a French programme on Thesiger? By Jean-Claude Luyat. Very well reviewed over there. Joe's girlfriend wrote to him about it.'

'I did actually, yes, Sam. Fortunately, our systems are not compatible, as I'm sure you know. Very expensive business, adapting tapes.'

'Nevertheless, reputations could have been... at stake?'

'Well, whatever. Gentlemen, can't we just get on with it?'

'Okay, Nick. Great idea.'

'Sam. Kingsley?'

'Well on the way. Can we have some location stuff in Africa?'

'No problem.'

'Ditto in South America, for Fawcett.'

'Yep. Geoff?'

'Iceland, please. That's all.'

'Great, everyone. You've probably all realised that the idea of a series is not on any more. There was simply no one else at the moment in a position to take anything on, and you've all made it clear that two pieces would have been too much to ask of you – and I entirely agree, on reflection. I mean, we'd just never have got it done, in terms of time alone. So, three programmes: Sam's; Geoff's; Nigel's. Oh, and by the way, Quent, who apologises for not being here – he's away filming up in Yorkshire – wondered if you might do an introductory together, if we can find an anchorman who would be acceptable to you all, someone perhaps like Lord Lincoln, if we can get him. You know, Randolph Julius. To chair it, and, sort of, hold the thing together. What d'you say?'

'Fine.'

'Nice thought, Nick.'

'Definitely.'

'Gentlemen, terrific! Thanks for coming. Details of location requirements and things to Vanessa here, okay darling?'

'Okay, Nick.'

*

'Sam? Sam Webster?'

'Speaking.'

'Jacquetta Rainsford.'

'Oh hello, what a nice surprise!'

'Listen, Sam. There's an old attic full of college junk that I had absolutely no knowledge of—'

'Good lord!'

'Exactly. Do you recall a house called Newnham Lodge, just round to the right and across the road, on our side I mean, from the bottom of Silver Street?'

'It belongs to Corpus. I had friends I used to visit there.'

'Right. And because it belongs to Corpus there's no obvious connection with us to speak of. But apparently, or so I'm told, a few years ago, when we reorganised and computerised the college library, Corpus offered to lend us the attic there to store some pretty superfluous junk we'd cleared out but were reluctant to get rid of irrevocably, if you see what I mean. And, Sam, it's all still there – oodles of it so they say. Virtually forgotten about by pretty well everyone.'

'Can you get at it?'

'Trust me, buster.'

'Oh, I will, believe me. Supposing I came up for the weekend? Could we go through it together?'

'You'd better bring some grotty old things to wear. It'll be pretty scungy up there, at a guess.'

'And this time I buy you lunch, okay?'

'*Andouillette* and chips', said Jacquetta Rainsford.

'Lots of chips, with Dijon mustard, green salad and a bloody great carafe of red wine.'

Part Three

The Bakhtiari Document

Chapter One

They stood together on the threshold of the attic at Newnham Lodge and took in the apparent chaos of tea chests, shrouded shapes and all the other miscellaneous clutter that lay gathering dust before them.

'Hell's bells!' said Sam.

'Precisely,' said Jacquetta Rainsford.

'The accumulated clutter of college life over tracts of time.'

'Aeons, yes.'

'What precisely is an aeon?'

'I'll tell you later. If we're going to go in for that kind of thing we'll be here for ever, so let's get started. We must be systematic, thorough and fast, and I suggest that we begin by deciding, more or less anyway, what it is we think we're looking for.'

Despite the froth, the bubble and the chatter, the mischievous glint and the delicious smile, there was an incisive, unsentimental quality to her mind which, more than anything else, brought back to Sam the sense of what this place had been for him; he acknowledged it with something like joy.

'We are looking, at a guess, for some kind of cache of written material – letters, a journal, perhaps. I'm not sure. Basically, just anything to do with Eleanor Tew which may throw light on the matter of her disappearance one way or another.'

'So, we'll look in boxes and suitcases? Trunks and things?'

'Pretty well everywhere and in anything that isn't quite obviously a waste of time.'

'Things can get put in wrong places, you know.'

'Okay, we look in everything. Half the total space each.'

'Right, let's mark the divide down the middle like this, then you take one side and I'll take the other.'

'Jacquetta?'

'Yes?'

'I don't know how to thank you for this. I mean, any of it. Whether we're successful or not.'

'I may contrive to think of some way for you to do so in due course. But let's get on with it now. We could be up here all day, and it's not so cosy, is it? I mean, did it ever strike you how sheer sodding cold Cambridge is in the winter? Why anyone should choose to put a university down here in the middle of the Fens I cannot imagine.'

'There must have been a reason—'

'Of course there must, and one could find out what it was, if one could be bothered. As it is, I'm rather more interested in the Countess of Alès at the moment.'

'Who?'

'The Countess of Alès. An androgynous person who used to dress up in man's clothes and fight duels, since she rather fancied herself as an artist of the blade. Which she was, too.'

'How extraordinary.'

'Yes. She was actually more a case for a psychologist than a historian. She always won her duels and she always killed to do so, which one didn't invariably, you know. With the same thrust in every instance, as far as I can ascertain, exactly placed between a certain two ribs. The woman must have had a wrist like a universal joint. And the killing was… strange, like a ritual enactment of some dreadful secret symbolism. I'll bet she came as she scored, if you see what I mean.'

'I do. Is this the world of *Liaisons Dangereuses*?'

'It is. Precisely.'

'What strange and unattractive things you know about, madam. Odd thing, though, androgyny.'

'Not really. Just one of nature's many anomalies. But what the mind makes of it – that's where the fun begins.'

'True, I suppose. Some chaps really get turned on by boyish women, you know. Not that I would claim to be one…'

'No, I'd rather inferred that—'

'But you think there was some kind of erotic thing involved, do you, with your countess?'

'I suspect so. I keep intending to talk to Nicky. She's our psychologist as well as my best friend in college, but I haven't got round to it yet. How d'you imagine this got here? Horrible thing!'

'An elephant's foot waste bin? A relic of Empire, I'd say. Some proud lady of the college no doubt once accompanied her diplomatic or military husband and family to far-flung parts and brought it home eventually as from some protracted grand tour.'

'Nothing there. I've been through all this lot now, and I'm marking what I've done with dust sheets bundled up like this.'

'Nice work.'

They worked on, through lunchtime and into the afternoon, Jacquetta's *andouillette* and chips repeatedly postponed, until at length…

'God, I'm so hungry! I'm simply going to have to stop and get something to eat. Even the pub sandwiches across the road will be finished now. You must know what Cambridge is like in term-time. Everything gets bloody well eaten every day and very fast. Honestly, it's like a plague of locusts. Lovely bread buns, with pâté and salad and egg mayonnaise, and fishy things, like tuna and prawns in aïoli and… Sam!'

'Just a second.'

'No! Come and see!'

'What is it?'

'Just come here, would you?'

Something in her voice told him what he was still not quite ready to believe.

'You've found it, haven't you?'

'Yes,' said Jacquetta. And she burst into tears.

'My darling girl,' said Sam, and he took her in his arms and kissed her properly for the first, marvellous time.

It was a brown cardboard box of the office stationery type, rectangular and quite deep. It sat, with a kind of complacent inevitability all of its own, at one end of a metal shelf belonging to a stack constructed out of something like an overgrown Meccano set, most of which remained draped in dust sheets beyond the point to which Jacquetta had uncovered it. On one end of the box, plainly visible, was a label which read: C.E. de G. TEW, 1872–75. Opened, the box proved to contain letters, papers and, most thrilling of all, a fat volume bound in heavy leather, with a rusting clasp.

'Oh, my God!' said Sam. 'That's been in water. What about the ink inside?'

'It's all right. There are ways of deciphering water-stained manuscripts, even when the ink has run.'

'May we remove this?'

'As long as I take responsibility for it and tell the Principal, yes.'

'Right, then what I suggest is that we tidy up here, what there is to do anyway, then go and have sausage, egg and chips or something like that as nearby as we can find—'

'Lorry drivers' caff just down the road.'

'Excellent. Then we go straight to the Garden House—'

'What? Like this?'

'Like what?'

'Well, just look at us!'

Sam looked and noticed the cobwebs in her hair, the dust on her jumper and jeans, the smudge on one cheek.

'Yes,' he said, 'why not? Anyway, I did actually book a room there with a bathroom.' He looked at her and swallowed hard.

'A double room,' he said with his heart in his mouth.

For an interminable moment they faced each other across the attic in the fading light of the late afternoon. Afterwards, it was the absolute stillness of it that he remembered, as hope flickered, the possibility of renewal.

'You dirty old sod!' said Jacquetta Rainsford.

'I was rather hoping that you might prove to be a dirty young sod,' he said, easily now.

'Oh, I am,' she said. 'Believe me, I really, really am.'

★

Much later, Sam said, 'I have to go to Africa. We're starting on the location stuff for my Kingsley film the week after next. Swamps, canoes, crocodiles and things.'

'And how long will it all take?'

'No idea. It could be April before it's all in the can.'

'I shall be in Aix-en-Provence.'

'Your countess?'

'Exactly.'

'Couldn't we meet up somewhere? Could you, say, get across to Venice for a bit?'

'Oh, wow! Brilliant. I think I just might manage that, yes. "But this all pleasures fancies bee". Yes, a long weekend's... fucking... in the bosom, so to speak, of the Serenissima herself would be just the ticket. A weekend

long screw, a socking great *aargh* protracted in juddering
slow motion all up and down the length of the snaky-waky
old Grand Canal itself. Can you imagine the sheer... tickle
of it? But of course! You're the old Ticklebeast himself,
aren't you, Sam? I've just been shafted by the Ticklebeast!
How absolutely marvellous! And the food's pretty nice too
in Venice. *Alla veneziana. Fegato alla veneziana* and... things.
Oh, isn't life sometimes simply gorgeous? It is gorgeous,
isn't it? Don't you think it's all absolutely... gorgeous, Sam?
Don't you?'

'Yes.'

'You know, for a writer you are remarkably laconic. Sex
always makes me talkative.'

'I'd noticed.'

'Yes, well. I get some of my best ideas when I'm being
fondled by a nice feller, because, with me, it stimulates the
mind as well as the body, and, whilst I'm on the subject, I
simply must say, sir, that I have never been quite so
knowingly handled as just now. It really was excruciatingly,
exquisitely... thing! You know?'

'I do.'

'Oooh, good. Yes, knowingly, that's the word. My
French aristocrats were good at love too, you know. They
had the time and space to make a thing of it all, so they did.
And they were knowing about... carnality, like the *Kama
Sutra* and you. I say, you know, I've often had the thought
that there must be loads of really terrific filth lying around
in the archives of France all over the place. Things pro-
scribed by the Church and all that. D'you think I should
research it? Jacquetta Rainsford on mucky French books? I
could beef up the title of the topic suitably with a spot of
nifty rhetoric, so that the university – this univarsitah –
would endorse the project, then I could produce a coffee-
table alternative which would actually be the real thing, if
you see what I mean, for drooling over, with incredibly

rude illustrations: "Oh, I say, just look at this one!" she said, choking genteelly over her digestive biscuit... Because, the thing is, you can do it absolutely anywhere and anyhow, can't you? On the sofa or over an armchair, in the back of a car, standing up in a hammock, on the hostess trolley, up a pear tree, on the kitchen table—'

'Darling, do be quiet,' said Sam.

'I'm sorry, Sam, but I'm totally zonked. What with the search first, then that tea, then you, and all the rest of it – it was absolutely lovely but I just can't take it and my mind races, I can't stop it. I'll be getting hysterical next.'

'Then lie in my arms and close your eyes.'

'Mmm! Heaven. How absolutely, absolutely, gorgeous!'

And within minutes, as, outside, the February dawn broke palely over the Fens and down the Grantchester reaches of the Cam, they both slept.

From 'A Persian Expedition'

Sunrise. As we emerge from the deep slumber of sheer physical exhaustion, golden sunlight sweeps majestically down the flank of a nearby hill and makes towards us like an incoming tide. Our flocks are already on the move among the rocks that strew the hillside under the oaks. Too soon the morning sun will blaze, throwing blue shadows on distant snow-capped mountains. Around me now there is animated movement as camp is struck yet again and the inevitable daily round of the constant search for pasture begins. Ahead of us lies a steep pass to be climbed, with the correspondingly precipitate descent on the far side, down into a stretch of ravine where we plough through the mud. By the time we reach the far end, the river, jade green, will flicker in the heat of the high midday sun. Thus we pursue our ways through this wild and beautiful country. One starts at dawn; one stops at dusk. In the evening there will be fire, a beast from the flock slaughtered fresh to eat, water from the spring to drink with the meat, perhaps a story to follow the meal. Then sleep, in readiness for another similar day to follow...

★

'Oh, wow!' said Jacquetta. 'Wow, wow!' Then, 'Sam?'

'Yes?'

'Can you imagine how this has lain untouched by human hand, mouldering away in this box here in the college for more than half a century?'

'I can,' he said evenly, his equanimity highlighting her impatience.

'But doesn't it just make you wonder what else there must be, lying about all over the place? Do you remember how Eco invented the lost second book of Aristotle's *Poetics*, the one on comedy, in that novel—'

'*The Name of the Rose.*'

'That's it! What I mean is that it's all perfectly plausible, isn't it? When you come across something like this?'

'True, darling. But one hardly does it all the time.'

'Just as well – one could hardly live with the sheer excitement of it. It's fantastic, isn't it? Those opening lines! One is there, with her. I reckon that what you've found here knocks my androgynous countess into a cocked tricorne hat!'

'You found it, sweetie. I didn't.'

'You pursued it, Sam. I found it for you because I wanted you to have it. And to have me too, I must add.'

'I knew that, darling.'

'Did you really? Yes, of course you did. I knew you knew. God! It's all quite... brilliant, isn't it? Eleanor Tew. And you and me.'

Sam stood up and walked away from the table where they had been working together, across to the window looking down into the college garden. He was a novelist again, and a lover. He would write the story of Eleanor Tew, and he would feast on Jacquetta and she upon him, 'as these lovers do,' again and again. The possibility of renewal, that faint trace he had sensed in the instant she had first turned to welcome him to the library had proved true.

154

'Yes,' he said, 'It is brilliant. Triff 'n' brill!'

'How do you know that? Oh, sorry, what a daft question to ask of a novelist!'

'No, no,' he said. 'It's a perfectly reasonable question. The answer's Joe. It's the kind of thing he used to say. You're Joe's age,' he said, with a tremor of apprehension.

'So what? You're an incredibly dishy middle-aged novelist. Shall we get on with it?'

★

…As a small child at home in the nursery in Leamington Spa I used to dream a vision of high and lonely places, of a mountainous landscape against which there moved, across swift-flowing, icy rivers and over formidable gradients of scree and similar rocky wastes, a concatenation of figures both animal and human. They moved apparently raggedly and yet clearly with some collective purpose in mind, and now, here in the Bakhtiari mountains, I have become a part of that collective purpose, in a manner which I shall duly explain. I am one of the human figures in that landscape, and, now that I am dying – for the signs that this is the case are not to be denied – I wish to set my thoughts in order in the hope that, one way or another this, my account of my Persian expedition, will perhaps reach the attention of those I would care to have read it. When it is as complete as may be, I shall hand it to one of the boys of the tribe and have him trade it, with a European if possible and if not with whomsoever, for artefacts of a kind to be of use to all. A cooking pot of metal such as the gypsies make, a supply of nails, a set of stirrups will be a fair exchange. Such a trade, of the thing I have made, would be gratifyingly apt, a real contribution on my part to the collective purpose. For in composing this narration I have to allow that I have had a secondary purpose – one that has been wholly self-interested and which is now, fortunately, all but fulfilled – upon which I have insisted to myself no matter what and, most particularly, in despite of the subordinate place, as a woman, which I have readily assumed within the tribe. This purpose has been no other than to preserve my own sense of who I am through the regular use of my native language, as well as to counter in myself the mundane weariness which dogs my dear friends all the while as they trudge their way with their flocks.

In the time I have been with my nomads, I have learned to converse in their tongue; indeed more, to live in it, and, as I have become increasingly proficient in that tongue, so I have become accessible to them and even, I may say, one of them. Here I recall two things, one both amusing and yet poignant, since it concerns my dear dead brother, William, whose admiration for his first commanding officer, Captain Nicholas Duvivier, was tempered only by his bewilderment at the captain's ability to speak a number of out-of-the-way dialects which in fact belonged to approximately this part of the globe. 'Extraordinary noises the feller can make,' he would say. 'Most extraordinary!' And I recall, too, Willie's bemused reference to my father's attempt to explain to him and to my other brother, Fred, how the 'noises' might well add up, despite their ostensibly unfamiliar qualities, to something as familiar, indeed as mundane, as our own English tongue might seem to him. 'Oh, absolutely, Father!' I can hear William say now, using the formula he always did when agreement was clearly expected of him without his quite being able to understand why: 'If you say so, sir.' How desolating a thought, that dear, dear Willie should be no more, that the planet should be rolling on its way as though he had never existed. But how truly my father put the matter. For the 'extraordinary noises' of the Bakhtiari dialect do indeed add up to nothing more than he had apprehended.

156

The other, second thing is of relevance to my present situation for somewhat different reasons. I recall the long and instructive conversations which took place subsequently between my uncle, Count Hubert de Granville, and myself on our walks in the forest at Le Molay in 1877, now nearly ten years ago...

*

'Hah!' said Sam.

'Nice one,' said Jacquetta.

*

...He it was who first spoke to me of the nomads of this part of the world and who tactfully invited me to consider the nature of the challenge involved in adapting to conditions of life so different and even opposite from what I knew, conditions even more repugnant, in certain ways, than the constraints of social convention operative in the England of that time. I recall my rejoinder, to the effect that I should be an observer rather than a participant, and how naive that must have made me seem to him, so knowledgeable as he was in the ways of humankind. For over these last few years...

*

'Just a minute,' said Sam.

'She eventually left England in 1880,' said Jacqui Rainsford. 'At least, that's what you told me Mrs Barraclough told you in Warwick—'

'And she disappeared in 1882,' said Sam. 'Apparently there was contemporary stuff on it, remember? Newspaper features and things, prompted by the cessation of correspondence from her end with the friends like Anna Rowlandson with whom she was in contact.'

'Can we find an exact date here, anywhere?'

'If there is one it must be in the spoiled bit, I imagine.'

'Keep looking, though.'

'Oh, certainly, but let's just consider this a moment. She speaks of her "naivety", or what must have appeared as such to her French uncle when she insisted that she would observe rather than participate; she learned the nomad language sufficiently well to be anxious about preserving her knowledge of English as something vital to her sense of who she was—'

'She became a nomad woman,' said Jacquetta Rainsford. 'She severed her links with Europe and home – well, almost, except for this – and she became a nomad woman, having begun presumably by simply travelling with them.'

'Inference,' said Sam. 'And besides, she still writes as an English lady. Just consider: "upon which I have insisted to myself no matter what, and, most particularly, in despite of the subordinate place, as a woman, which I have readily assumed within the tribe".'

'Of course she does. In that sense she is still herself. She is two people.'

'I suppose that is possible.'

'Certainly it's possible – there are lots of instances of it. If we just examine that bit again, for a moment. She is intent upon continuing with the writing of her journal – this, after all, is her "Persian Expedition", isn't it? She is concerned to preserve her sense of who she is in the matter of an English identity. Her name must mean a very great deal to her in several ways. In the first instance, it signals and defines an individuality which she prizes almost above all things; in the second as a family thing – the Tews must surely have had something of that kind of pride about them, with the French lineage and the English gentility...

Because she would have acquired a nomad name, would she not, and with it a quite separate identity into which she willingly enters, given that she is clearly so very fond of her nomad "friends". And then there's the other thing...'

'Yes?'

'What was it she said? Oh yes, here: "to counter in myself the mundane weariness which dogs my dear friends all the while as they trudge their way with their flocks". Sam, how absolutely dreadful! They must exist, the nomads, in a state of constant exhaustion, dragging out an existence at the most basic level in the middle of this wild, tumbled, gorgeous mountain terrain. I'm not surprised that she made such efforts to distance herself somewhat, even though she loved them and identified with them and learned their language so she could be one of them.'

'Paradox and improbability,' said Sam. 'Your inferences are marvellous, darling, quite stunning, but these things are still extraordinarily difficult to reconcile.'

'That's the most interesting bit,' said Jacquetta. 'I mean, it's not to be doubted, any of this, is it?'

'No, it's not to be doubted. But someone like her? A dissident, a non-believer, a virtual lady pioneer in the cause of women's emancipation generally, who wrote her books, remember, who became what she did become specifically to make her contribution? And here we have her "readily assuming a subordinate place within the tribe"? It really is the most extraordinary paradox!'

'Perhaps not necessarily. So we'd better read on, hadn't we? Have you noticed how she draws on long-term recollections of England, that bit about her brother and Captain Thing and France with her uncle? It's as though she were clinging to an identity which might be beginning to slip away from her, especially now she knows she's dying, however she does know that. I find this very moving... And then the dream from the nursery! How do you explain that, for instance? Surely that is far more anomalous than the other thing? I could never hope to explain that, I think, although there may be psychologists who might claim to be able to. I must talk to Nicky: she knows about this kind of thing, as much as anyone does, that is.'

'Shall we get on with it?'

★

For over these last years, which I have spent continuously here in the fastness of the mountains, in remote and lonely places the existence of which was first made manifest to me in my childhood dream, among these primitive herdsfolk whom I have learned not only to love but also to identify with in the fullest degree, in admiration and wonder at the stoicism of a mode of existence, an acceptance of necessities of circumstance so cruel as to be unimaginable to any European, nurtured as we all are for the most part in a luxury of which my tribesfolk could not even dream, I have come to appreciate in real terms something of the marvellous resilience of the human intelligence in the ways it finds of adapting to the many and various modes of subsistence it is obliged by circumstance to evolve in the interests of its own survival and continuance. We are herdsfolk. Our flocks, the wealth of the tribe, are all and everything to us. We live constantly on the move, effectively bivouacking in rude, temporary structures, our black tents, thrown up for the night at the end of the travelling day. It is indeed in such a poor shelter that I write this now, by the guttering glimmer of a lamp of grease such, no doubt, as was already in use in Old Testament times. For the age-old cycle of our year is dictated, logically enough, by the need to find pastureland or at least minimal grazing for the animals; in the course of that year we traverse mountain ranges which force the most appalling risks upon us, six outwards and the same six back, that is for those who survive the final crossing, in the floods of spring melt water, of the River Bazuft. We are ten thousand years old collectively, we nomads, and thus it has always been and no doubt always will be. However, I know now, with my strength significantly ebbing from one day to the next, that this time I shall not survive the river crossing. With the old and the infirm, I shall simply be left behind; indeed, I shall choose to be left behind, to die as is the usage here since time immemorial, once one's effective contribution to the collective impulse to survive is no more. At the river crossing, boys become men and the useless are discarded so that the tribe may continue to exist one way or another.

This year, however, that time is not quite yet, and I must use the interim as best I may to fill out this record for whatever purpose. For my fellows do not write. Their collective memory is exclusively oral and to them the act of writing, exposed, might well appear a mystery full of threat and menace. So I write this secretly, while others around me sleep the sleep of physical exhaustion which invariably follows on from the exertions of the working day. But at night, here in the mountains, the cold is simply indescribable, the ground on which we lie as hard as iron. I am therefore able to pen my words only for the briefest of moments, owing to both the physical and moral conditions of existence. Ironically but necessarily, I have become Jane Austen, concealing her manuscript beneath the drawing-room cushions. For, as ladies were not expected to pursue such interests in the genteel society of the England of seventy years ago, how much less possible must it be for a nomad woman, whose function it is to produce men children, as I have done...

*

'There! I knew it!'

'Darling, how could you possibly—'

'It was the only possible reason for her to cut herself off so absolutely from someone like her father, whom she adored. I'll bet she had twin sons: twins run in families, don't they, and she did have twin brothers, remember? That would have given her enormous prestige within the tribe. So she chose to remain, to mother her Bakhtiari baby, or babies, then she was finally trapped by terminal disease.'

'And her lover? The father of her child?'

'She's not going to tell that. Why should she? A virile male figure silhouetted in the doorway of a tent at dusk – a hunter, a horseman, a shepherd. Hossein, Akhmed, Taha... We can't expect to learn that, Sam.'

'True. Anyway...'

'Anyway...'

★

...to produce men children, as I have done, to grow up to assume the shepherding of the herd once their progenitors have aged beyond what this requires of them, how much less possible must it be for such a woman, native born, to conceive of what might be involved in what I am about at this moment? In the particular circumstances so critically obtaining, there can be only one answer to this question...

★

'God!' said Jacquetta. 'The confidence of her! This is a marvellous woman, Sam, really and truly in the tradition of the best! I mean, the equanimity of it! She's so at home with it all, isn't she? Given that her daily chores would have involved baking bread in the biblical way, mending clothes, making yoghurt from the milk she would have taken with the other women from the herd? *She*, Sam. Eleanor Tew. An English lady. It really is the most terrific story. And fuck the Iron Duchess. Well no, perhaps not.'

'I beg your pardon?' said Sam.

'Sorry, the Senior Tutor. That woman. She has a somewhat Wellingtonian nose and invariably dresses in grey. So the little girls gang up behind her back—'

'I see. But, darling, concerning the other thing, do you mean to maintain that motherhood became the one supreme value in her life? After all that she was? Eleanor Tew? Surely not?'

'Wait a minute, Sam. Because that's not the right way to put it, it simply isn't. Consider it this way. Motherhood is a biological function which may or may not be fulfilled in exactly the same way as the capacity to father offspring may or may not be fulfilled in men. All the rest is merely cultural. But she's already answered you, Sam, in her phrase, "in the particular circumstances so critically obtaining". I mean, can you imagine Bakhtiari women, leading a life which has not changed in ten thousand years, *ten thousand years*, Sam, and the *Iliad's* less than three thousand years old, campaigning for the vote? The world just isn't made like that, *mon ami*. At its simplest level, this journal acknowledges that "there are more things in heaven and earth", *et cetera*. There was a price to her Persian adventure, and she paid it readily: the price of a truly loving identification, on their own terms because they could not possibly have understood hers, with what look like wretched people to us but were quite obviously not at all to her. If you can call it a price, that is. It doesn't look as if she would have called her Bakhtiari son "a price", does it? Just imagine her love for him, and for a husband who was a hunter, a marksman, a horseman of skill and daring, one who awoke everything in her that had remained merely latent and repressed in her Victorian English self. Unless she was simply raped, of course, although I think on balance not, don't you? Given the calm content of it all?'

'Christ, Jacquetta!'

'Well, I don't know what the answer is. Do you?'

'No, of course I don't. I must say though, Doctor Rainsford, I find you extremely plausible. And you don't stop at stark alternatives, do you?'

'I didn't imagine you would have wanted me to, not for a minute.'

'I wouldn't, although documentary realism coming so hard upon pure D.H. Lawrence did take me a bit unawares.'

'It's all in the day's work, buster. God, I'm hungry! Would you like lunch here, in college?'

'No, thank you. Let's have a pint and a sandwich down the road, then come straight back and get on with this.'

'Can we have a nice dinner somewhere tonight, d'you think?'

'Certainly. Supposing I ring The Green Man at Fareham and book a table? You know, or perhaps you don't, it used to be old Maurice Allington's place, and I gather it's as good as ever, although I haven't actually been there for ages.'

'Triff! God, Sam, I do so enjoy you!'

★

...for the style in which we live our lives is surely one which can have changed hardly at all since time im-memorial. 'And the father of our people, the hillman, Bakhtyar, came out of the fastness of the southern mountains in ancient times,' the legend runs, and, in the absence of any notion of how time may be objectively recorded and measured, one can only infer that what is in question must be thousands of years, though how many exactly it remains impossible to specify with accuracy. And yet, despite the

164

initial inconvenience of it all, and oh, the discomfort, the
misery, the shame and humiliation of it in the first instance
to one whose life had been lived in the lap of a luxury so
alien to those wretched in the material things of existence,
despite this inconvenience – for it was nothing more than
that – there was for me always a familiarity, a predictability
to the nomad ways for which I am quite unable to account,
any more than I can account for what I already knew from
my childhood dream. I surmise that this has to do with the
way in which memory must in part be an inherited function of the mind as well as an individual possession: it is
therefore a question of function and will one day no longer
be a mystery...

*

'She's just anticipated the theory of the collective
unconscious!' said Sam.

'By roughly twenty or thirty years, I'd say. True. Nice
one,' said Jacquetta. 'What a pity, Sam, that she didn't live
long enough to know Jung's work. Because when you think
of it, she could have lived into your early lifetime, couldn't
she? A white-haired old lady with a silver-topped stick and
a store of experience worth... libraries.'

'Freya Stark was ninety-six,' said Sam, 'when she died
last year.'

'Exactly. Eleanor Tew would have been ninety-six in
1948.'

*

...we live a life that is constantly on the move, the imperative of movement being determined by the need to find
grazing for the sheep and goats which constitute our tribal
estate. We follow a route into the mountains that is

predetermined, as one would expect, and, because we travel thus, we carry only what is immediately of need and portable. We manufacture nothing, trading as necessary for things beyond our competence to fashion for ourselves. The wonderful strength of the men is the safeguard of our continued existence, as indeed is the production of male children, who in their turn will guarantee the well-being of the next generation. But, for all the purposeful virtue of our splendid men, their daring whether on horseback or on foot, their matter-of-fact, strictly practical courage, their compendious familiarity with local conditions – over huge distances – of weather and terrain, and here I am vividly reminded of Ludwig Rendl...

★

'Now, who could he have been?'

'A mountain ranger,' said Sam, 'in the *Bavarian Journal*. The man who trained her and Miss Rowlandson and took them up to the rock. She admired him enormously, and precisely because what she discerned in him was a kind of knowledge that made for wisdom, which was what her father and his doctor friend, by their example from her earliest childhood, had taught her to revere above all things.'

'I see, yes,' said Jacquetta Rainsford. 'I'm so glad I met you, Sam. I really, really am.'

'Reciprocated, but let's go on.'

★

...for all the purposeful virtue, the nomad life is one which leads nowhere if not simply out and back again. And at the end of the journey so heroically accomplished there is... nothing. Only an immense, stoic resignation...

*

'What an utterly appalling thought! An existence dragged out in exhaustion over all the years of life, only to end in oblivion.'

'All life ends in oblivion, darling.'

'True, but how someone like her could contrive to endure such wretchedness—'

'This doesn't read as wretched, does it?'

'No, it doesn't. I thought I had the answer, with the child, but could that have been the whole truth of the matter? Surely not?'

'There are several other things, are there not?'

'Such as?'

'Perhaps the power of her feeling for the father of the child? She speaks with admiration of the men of the tribe, doesn't she? "Our splendid men", for instance. Then the fact of her illness, which effectively trapped her, whether she felt it that way or not – and it doesn't look as if she did. And one other thing – one thing above all—'

'I'm positively agog, Sam. Do go on.'

'The diary. The "Persian Expedition". Don't you see? She was the "incorrigible writer" all along! It's a reference, darling, to the *Bavarian Journal*. There's a bit there where Anna calls her an "incorrigible writer", then wonders aloud why it should be that writers require correction. Eleanor chides her over what she picks up as a conventional turn of phrase – it's all part and parcel of the verbal thing that goes on between them. They had a lot of fun together, with words.'

'Lovely!'

*

...Here, however, I allow myself to turn to the contemplation and consideration of my own life as I lived it prior to my departure into this wilderness, and, since a private journal and the end of a life are peculiarly appropriate to an assessment and a truth-telling, I make bold here to claim that in the nomad life I have found the metaphor for all human life which I so dimly set out to seek from my Cambridge days, my point being that the purposeful virtue exemplified in my dear father and Doctor Barnes, in Ludwig Rendl and the nomad herdsmen of the Bakhtiari is what is of greatest significance in earthly life, no matter what its end. Which brings me to my private dilemma. For me, Eleanor Tew, that purposeful virtue I have described above has consisted of the writing I have engaged upon both in my earlier books and in this, my Persian journal. I have already written of the place of women amongst the nomads and of the fact that I write *in camera*, as it were, in order not to give offence to those I have come to love as my own folk or to create apprehension in them. If, for whatever reason, I were prevented from writing... In theory, of course, I could leave the tribe, return to my Western identity as Eleanor Tew. But in practice, even if I were not in so enfeebled a state as to render such a course of action quite out of the question, there are other compelling reasons I should find it impossible to opt for that. I choose therefore to continue with this journal for as long as I am able, and to remain behind at the river crossing, which is now not long hence...

...Further to this, then, I needs must turn my mind now to the devising of a stratagem by which I may ensure the posthumous delivery of this journal, not to my family as would be customary, since the effect of such a testimony as this upon aged parents long since convinced of my previous demise may be easily imagined, but to Clough Hall in Cambridge, where it may take its place, to lie unread by my request, for fifty years in the archive of that society, to be perused eventually by whoever of the sorority may find herself disposed to engage upon such a task in that distant future...

★

'She's talking about me!' said Jacquetta, and her voice in its awe was hardly louder than a whisper. 'She's talking about me – she really is, Sam. Because no one else has read this, don't you see? If anyone had, her name would have been known, surely, to more people than just that little queer on the fringes of Bloomsbury.'

'Charles Lytton.'

'That's right. As it is, not one of the sodding sorority ever even bothered to take an interest, until now. Poor Eleanor. Poor, poor darling!'

'No, no. Not poor. Because she achieved her purpose, didn't she? The journal reached its destination exactly as she intended it should. I wonder how it got here, you know, I really do.'

'There may be indications.'

'True.'

★

...I shall therefore enclose, in the package containing this volume, a directive to whomsoever it may concern of Her Majesty's representatives, or even a fellow countryman resident in Shiraz, Isfahan or preferably Tehran, to the effect that the journal is to be conveyed unread into the hands of the Principal of Clough. Presumably, this will be feasible through the normal diplomatic channels of communication.

*

'Jacqui, we haven't looked at what else is in the cardboard box, have we?'

'Me first!'

'Oh no, you don't!'

'All right, half each. And mention anything of interest.'

'Such as, for instance, that this is not her handwriting?'

'Look for signatures, addresses and references to her.'

'A lot of this is Rowlandson stuff – letters from Anna to friends – though why they should be in the Tew box—'

'Irrelevant for the moment. But there may be a reference to Eleanor's disappearance. Look for anything dated 1882.'

'Here's something,' Sam said at last. 'Listen to this:

There is still no news of my dear Eleanor, and since that correspondence pursued on such a regular basis between us has now effectively ceased to exist, given the protracted absence of response from her, I fear she may have fallen victim to all that may be most untoward, in view of the very great risk of her undertaking to venture effectively unaccompanied into regions so remote and inaccessible. There has been some mention of her disappearance in the public prints, and of course poor Mr Tew has been indefatigable in his investigation of all conceivable avenues of enquiry, but my poor Eleanor was not yet, alas, of sufficient consequence for the newspaper reportages to have amounted to anything very much more than a passing acknowledgement of the very real hazards of venturesome travel by ladies of delicate nurture, who would do better to remain in unhazardous domesticity as ladies properly should…

What a pair they must have made! I suppose it's all there, in the *Bavarian Journal*, in the description of the dinner party in Belgravia, for instance.'

'What?'

'Sorry. There's a most amusing account of their eve-of-departure-for-Munich dinner party at the Rowlandsons. However, that's about it, I suppose.'

'Two things missing.'

'Yes?'

'The "directive" she speaks of, you know, the "To Whom It May Concern" thing that was to be enclosed in the package containing the journal—'

'And?'

'A Foreign Office letter, or the letter of some agency covering the delivery of the document into the hands of the Principal here at Clough.'

'The first will be lost beyond retrieval.'

'And the second?'

'That will be right at the bottom of this box.'

But it was not.

'Never mind,' said Sam. 'I could almost write it myself.'

'Go on then,' said Jacquetta. 'I dare you!'

Sam looked up in the way middle-aged men do, removing the spectacles he wore for reading as he did so.

'Dear Madam,' he said, 'I am requested by His Excellency the Ambassador of Her Britannic Majesty at this embassy to convey into your hands the accompanying document, which has been delivered into the care of Her Majesty's Diplomatic Corps through the agency of Mr Hezekiah Dooks, an English tradesman and merchant currently resident in Isfahan—'

'What for?'

'Buying carpets to sell at home.'

'Of course. Sorry, go on.'

'Apparently Mr Dooks, in pursuit of his commercial purposes, was intercepted upon a lonely road in one of the most inaccessible regions in the south-west of this country by a native urchin of the most wretched, ragged kind, a child of nomads who, it would seem, most earnestly urged his noisome, sheepskin wrapped package upon Mr Dooks, who, on the point of sending the boy about his business, was arrested in his intention by, first, the obvious and by now tearful desperation of the little heathen, unintelligible in speech as he was, and, second, by the appearance among the contents of the package, which, in the vehemence of his efforts at persuasion, the boy had allowed to fall open, of a folded scrap of paper on which, to his utter amazement, he discerned in English the phrase: "To Whom It May Concern…" Do you see, darling?'

'Yes,' said Jacquetta Rainsford, 'I see.'

And she smiled her delicious smile.

★

…The moment of the river crossing is now imminent, and my own strength grows less and less. Once again I recall the words of my Uncle Hubert in the woods at Le Molay, when he spoke to me for the first time of these dear people amongst whom I am now living out the last days of my life. I remember too that, when he spoke to me of the matter of death, I was taken unawares, since this was not something to which I had as yet felt the necessity to give much consideration, in view of the cushioned security of my life as Eleanor Tew of Leamington Spa and Clough Hall, Cambridge.

Here, from the beginning of my association with the tribe, conditions of life have been very different, with deadly hazard a frequent factor to be contended with in the everyday course of a collective life lived constantly on the move over hard, demanding, unyielding terrain in regions – of mountain and plain – baking hot during the daytime and excruciatingly, freezingly cold at night. In such conditions, however, the health of the body becomes honed to a fine degree of rude well-being such as I simply do not recall having experienced in my life as a European. For the tribe on the move operates as a collective entity: its eyes are the eyes of each of its individual members, its continued safe keeping the concern of each and every one of us. And from this physical state of being, fostered by the imperatives of survival and the availability of only the roughest and most basic kinds of sustenance, there derives a sense of contentment as unimaginable, I surmise, to a rich European as the life of such a European would be to a tribesman of whatever age. I count myself as having lived a life of privilege effectively inestimable for having enjoyed the experience of both worlds, with awareness of the one enhancing that of the other.

To my kinsfolk, friends and acquaintances in Europe, I should, of course, long since have become unrecognisable, even before the onset of this wasting sickness which has so remorselessly deprived me of body and strength. It is a sadness, this, I have to allow, but fortunately I have been spared what I could scarcely have found a way to bear – the loss of mind. I am indeed more lucid, more essentially, characteristically myself even now, at this moment, as, having written through the night, I realise that I am very nearly at the end of my strength and therefore unable, now, to continue...

One recollection, however, does come back to me with vivid force. I recall, from Bavaria, from the moment when Ludwig Rendl led us, my dear Anna and myself, out onto the bare rock of the mountain, the urge, which I did not then indulge, to shout out my name, in some kind of triumph I surmise, some kind of celebration of everything that was uniquely me and not another being, Eleanor Tew! I am Eleanor Tew!...

★

'Go on,' whispered Jacquetta.

'That's it,' said Sam, the words coming more brusquely than he had intended.

'Nothing more?'

'Nothing more, no.'

'You know, Sam, she even got the last full stop in.'

'Effectively, yes. This is a natural ending, if ever there were one. Look, darling.'

Together they examined the gracious, faded, cursive script which Sam had first encountered in the inscription on the flyleaf of Anna's copy of the *Bavarian Journal* at the Barracloughs' in Warwick, tangible witness to the unique identity of a being who, at once exceptional and brilliant and mightily endowed, had found her place, in joy and contentment, amongst one of the most humble peoples of the earth.

'And the manner of her dying?' she asked eventually.

'That hardly bears thinking about.'

'Alone. In that wilderness. Like an animal.'

'With the stoic and proper dignity of one,' he said. 'In a hollow among the boulders perhaps; at the foot of a gigantic scree, with the river in full spate only yards away. Or curled up in the shade of a tree at the edge of a rock-strewn pasture, with the current nearby crashing its way over stony shallows and the spray dazzling silver in the bright sunlight. There. Alone. With her pain. And once beyond it, gradually, imperceptibly fading into oblivion, as the setting sun flushed great granite cliffs to shades of pink and lilac, deepening, in such hollows as were visible, to purest tones of blue. And as a serene immensity began to pervade that world of which she was now no longer a living part.'

Envoi

Voices

Chapter One

The raw cold of Cambridge in the early part of the new year gave way to the milder climate of the Thames Valley at Kew in mid-March, as Jacquetta Rainsford travelled up to London to spend a few days with Sam in Haverfield Gardens prior to his departure for Africa.

'I shall cook for us,' she said. 'It's still sharp enough for a spot of *la grosse cuisine de la campagne*, don't you think? Let's have a savoury stew, with gobbets of everything, a *pot au feu à la française*.'

'Sounds terrific. You know, darling, a month from now the whole street will be a riot of cherry blossom. Can you imagine?'

'Yes, I can. Because Sidgwick Avenue will be the same.'

'True. That's how I remember it. Quite different from how it was the day we met. Which reminds me. Do you think you could keep your eyes open around Cambridge, in David's or wherever, for a copy of the *Pyrenean Excursion*? Since you're so good at rooting things out?'

'Certainly. I already have, in fact.'

It was a companionable thing, to be in a position to prolong the kind of exchanges they had entered into from the start over Eleanor Tew here, in his own house in Haverfield Gardens. Novel too, for him, after several years of solitary living punctuated only by the occasional brief liaison as well as the periodic thunderous incursions from Joe, which, of late, had become similarly irregular. For her, after the intensive and purposeful years of Tripos, doctorate and fellowship election, the talk was the more enjoyable for being casual.

*

'You know, Sam,' she said one evening as they chopped vegetables together and shared a bottle of Ventoux in the kitchen, 'I don't think I should ever want to live with anyone on a long-term basis: I'm too attached to myself and my own purposes, my research and the books I plan to write. How about you?'

'Not any more,' said Sam. 'My marriage to Claire was a good one for as long as it lasted, and there was Joe, of course. A gigantic little boy, crashing about the house in a suit of plastic armour. But it was another life, when all's said and done. And I have to say that I am more content now, more my own man than I have ever been. I'm fifty-two and I intend to write a dozen more novels. You know, after *Ticklebeast*, when I couldn't get anything going and had to resort to commissions for documentary films, I thought I'd had it. And I was still thinking I'd had it when I met you. Then, when we found the Tew material and started to work on it together, I quite suddenly realised that I'd been right to follow up Lytton's reference because there would be a novel of some kind to be written round the story of Eleanor, and I was the man to do it. So, I was still a novelist, and still a lover, what is more. I was looking down into the garden over towards the tennis courts at Clough and I was aware that I still had the scent of you on me, because I hadn't wanted to wash you away: as far as such a thing is possible, it was an utterly timeless moment.'

'I'm delighted to have been of service. I suppose the novel is the right form for it, isn't it? For the story, I mean. There being so little to go on actually, in the way of material, I mean. Apart from the diary and Anna's letters.

And with there being so little in print either, leaving out that *Tatler & Bystander* thing from 1880-whenever it was and a couple of newspaper references. Which makes me wonder – and I've been meaning to ask you about this – how was it that Lytton felt obliged to make what he did of her disappearance? How did he even know of it? Because his reference in *Eminent Adventurers* was something decidedly more, wasn't it, than merely academic?'

'He was family,' said Sam. 'Well, sort of.'

'You never told me that.'

'I'm sorry. I thought I had. His mother was a Hebblethwaite.'

'Remind me.'

'Anna Rowlandson, remember, married a Reverend Jonathan Hebblethwaite—'

'And died in childbirth having produced George, who was named at her wish after her military brother, who had been killed in action at Isandhlwana at the same time as his boon companion, William Tew. Yes?'

'Right. Lytton, it appears, was fathered by the son of an older Hebblethwaite sister. Must have been quite a lot older, unless Mr Hebblethwaite himself was relatively advanced in years at the time of his marriage to Anna, which is perfectly possible, of course.'

'And the date of Lytton's book?'

'Oh, 1925-ish. It all fits. Mrs Barraclough made it all quite clear, though she clearly had very little time for Lytton. 'A horrible little man,' she called him.'

'Lovely! One can see why, of course.'

'One can.'

'Oh, this is nice! Being here, I mean. Isn't it nice? Don't you think it's nice?'

'I think it's... incredibly—'

'Nice?'

'Tremendously nice.'

'This Ventoux's pretty nice, too. You really go for these southern ones, don't you, Sam? I've noticed. You've got Gigondas, Fitou, Côtes de Provence—'

'That's because I can't afford the great clarets and burgundies—'

'No, it isn't. It's because you like them. Do you recall, sir, our first carnal encounter at the Garden House?'

'I most earnestly hope never to forget it as long as I live.'

'Oooh, good! Because for me, I must say, it gave a wholly new resonance to the phrase "Stap me vitals!" If you see what I mean?'

'I... just might.'

'You were brilliant. So loving and... knowingly considerate. I mean, having been bonked – which is just about it, really, bonked – all over the place in a variety of ways by several of the more or less rough young beasts who slouch about Cambridge on the lookout for it more or less all the time, which is not to say that I haven't spent a certain amount of time on the lookout for it too, don't get me wrong... and if you get my meaning? But you were brilliant! I was thinking though, you know, Sam, about the metaphor of nomad life, because it struck me on reflection how very appropriate it was not only to Eleanor Tew, but to us as well. I am a nomad, basically. A middle-class nomad. I put my work first, as the Bakhtiari put their flocks first, and so do you. It is, after all, the only right way of the world.'

'True, darling.'

'And in the meantime, since I am beginning to burble, we can shut up and wallow in carnal delight, an' all that, can't we?'

'Certainly we can. But we can take our time over it too, don't you agree? And think about it, relish the prospect... and things?'

'As I relish the prospect of meeting you in Venice in a month or so. Could we open another bottle, d'you think, and make a start on that garlic pâté?'

Chapter Two

'"The Pursuit of Swamps",' said Sam, 'or, "Coming Across Crocodiles". My titles, her text. Just listen, Quent.'

'This is a fascinating pursuit. For people who like that sort of thing, it is just the sort of thing they like, as the art critic of a provincial town wisely observed anent an Impressionist picture recently acquired for the municipal gallery. But it is a pleasure to be indulged in with caution; for one thing, you are certain to come across crocodiles. Now, a crocodile drifting down in deep water or lying asleep with its jaws open on a sandbank in the sun, is a picturesque adornment to the landscape when you are on the deck of a steamer, and you can write home about it and frighten your relations on your behalf; but when you are away among the swamps in a small dugout canoe, and that crocodile and his relations are awake... and when he has got his foot upon his native heath – that is to say, his tail within holding reach of his native mud – he is highly interesting, and you may not be able to write home about him—'

'Priceless,' said Quentin Rodgers, as Sam switched off the cassette player. 'What an extraordinary lady!'

'Totally unflappable,' said Sam. 'A teller of tall tales, one who was not disinclined to embroider upon the truth somewhat, a trickster, a—'

'Liar?'

'A teller of tales. I thought, you see, that if there were to be any radio back-up to the series, a few words in place might not come amiss, so I did this.'

'Good. Could be useful. Where's it from, that crocodile stuff?'

'The *Travels in West Africa.*'

'Date?'

'1897.'

'Bit close to Fawcett?'

'Not really. Different era, different continent.'

'True. May I have another?'

'Help yourself.'

'Thanks. You might care to know, by the way, that it's absolute mayhem on the home front.'

'At ITE? Hopley?'

'Precisely.'

'I thought there must be something doing. Geoff and I both did. He was positively incandescent over Saggers.'

'I'm not surprised. The whole thing was pretty inept on Nick's part.'

'So it was him?'

'Absolutely. Because there are reasons which I won't go into why Hopley is not exactly the flavour of the month at ITE. So, when hints of modifications to the management structure began to edge themselves his way, he decided to flex a spot of political-type muscle and got Saggers in on the project. Met him at somebody's dinner table; you know how it is, got on affably enough – no small achievement I imagine, though I gather from what he said that he caught Saggers in a good mood. Perhaps he'd just autographed the fifty millionth copy of his last effort on behalf of his party – and bingo! But he'd never have got anything done, you know. Hadn't the know-how and couldn't be bothered to do anything about it, being the sort of writer, if that's the word, who uses teams of minions to do that sort of thing for him. There would have been no personal stamp on it, if you see what I mean, because he hasn't got a personal stamp as far as I can see. There just isn't anything in the way of value-coloured perception in any of the drivel he churns out... So of course he pulled out; it never was remotely his sort of thing. And that's another thing. People talk, of course. ITE's a beehive, it positively buzzes. It got around that Saggers was doing a travel thing for Hopley, with Webster, Hayward and Wheatley, and people couldn't believe it: they laughed, they roared, they absolutely fell about! I mean, you know, the thought of that pinstriped little berk proposing to do... Thesiger, for Christ's sake! Thesiger! In a series team with guys like you three, to boot! The whole thing was quite priceless, but it did Nick's reputation for judgement no good at all. You only need one clanger like that, at ITE, you know, and you're rapidly down the doodah! There are just too many sharp fellers lurking round the corner – and rightly so, I say. It makes for a good company.'

'I'm glad that Frenchman did Thesiger, though. I'd love to see that.'

'Luyat? It was absolutely brilliant. I loved it. Saw it at a girlfriend's in Saint Cloud.'

'Anyway Quent, we're well on the way now, thanks mainly to you.'

'Oh, pooh! I must admit, it is bloody hard work out here. Thank Christ for air-conditioning and scotch, eh? Listen, Sam, whilst I think about this, how does the, at present somewhat faint possibility, of a TV film of *Ticklebeast* grab you? For some time in the future. After all, one does hope to move up the hierarchy in due course.'

'I see. With a quality cast?'

'As good as we could afford.'

'Right. Of course it grabs me, Quent. How could it not? It'll grab Julian too. Julian Rosenberg. My agent.'

'Right. Then we must keep in touch. We could have a lot of fun with a satirical look at the City, and it could be made to look absolutely stunning... Yes, definitely!'

'May I play you a bit more of this?'

'Do, Sam. Then I'm off.'

'Listen. This is madam on "the whiteman's grave".'

'I enquired of all my friends, as a beginning, what they knew of West Africa. The majority knew nothing. A percentage said: "Oh, you can't go there! That's where Sierra Leone is – the white man's grave, you know". If these were pressed further, one occasionally found that they had relations who had gone out there after having been "sad trials", but, on consideration of their having left not only West Africa but this world, were now forgiven and forgotten. One lady, however, kindly remembered a case of a gentleman who had resided some few years at Fernando Po, but when he returned, an aged wreck of forty, he shook so violently with ague as to dislodge a chandelier, thereby destroying a valuable tea service and flattening the silver teapot in its midst.'

'Priceless,' said Quentin Rodgers. 'And thereby hangs a theme, what is more. If the most hideous of transgressions is to disrupt the proprieties no matter what mayhem is being perpetrated outside in the street or wherever... Do you see?'

'I do', said Sam. 'Good!'

'D'you know, I'd no idea Kingsley was so droll. I can see why you chose her. Reminds me of Fanny Burney. I mean, girls like that – or perhaps one should say "gels" – are really quite something, aren't they?'

'Yes,' said Sam, 'they are.'

And in the air-conditioned anonymity of his hotel room, a pinpoint of light in the deep, deep darkness of the tropics, he thought of Eleanor Tew and Anna Rowlandson, of Emma Rosenberg, Maria Brooke, Jacquetta Rainsford...

Chapter Three

'Good evening, viewers. My name is Randolph Julius Lincoln, and in the studio with me now I have three writers who are all very different from each other but who have been brought together by Independent Television Enterprises to script an individual contribution to a new short series of films on travel and travellers. Going clockwise round the table then, on my immediate left is Sam Webster, novelist and author of, amongst other titles, the prizewinning *Ticklebeast* – wonderful title, Sam, love to ask you about that some time. Sam is also a maker of documentary films, mostly on the subject of travel, well, no, that's not perhaps quite accurate but, anyway, his last success, though for a rival concern, ha, ha! was a splendid piece on the transhumant shepherds of Provence, and his contribution to the current series is to be a film, most of which is already in the can – am I not right, Sam? – on Mary Kingsley, of whom more later. And, coming round the table then, next is Nigel Wheatley, youngest contributor and best-selling author of a highly entertaining account of fieldwork, social anthropological fieldwork that is, carried out for purposes of academic research amongst the…?'

'M'bhutu.'

'…As you say, Nigel, the M'bhutu; also of West Africa, although of a very different part of that vast region from that travelled by Sam's intrepid Victorian lady. The title of Nigel's book is appropriately enough, *Notes From the Back of Beyond* and it is, I can assure you, viewers, a most entertaining read. Nigel's contribution to the series took him to a completely different continent, to South America in fact, to make a film on Peter Fleming's search for Colonel Fawcett, whose unexplained disappearance in 1924, somewhere in the Mato Grosso most likely, constitutes a notorious incident in the annals of travel. The Case of the Vanishing Colonel. And now to number three in this team of globe-trotting, film-making wordsmiths, Geoffrey Hayward, linguist and adventurer, whose love affair with the frozen north – pretty well lifelong, I should imagine, Geoff? – resulted in the publication last year of *Following the Reindeer*, a fascinating account of time spent with the nomad Lapps of the Arctic Circle. Constantly on the move, I should imagine, Geoff?'

'Constantly, Julius. Yes.'

'And Geoffrey Hayward's contribution to this series is to be a film on William Morris's travels in Iceland in the 1870s. Right, Geoff?'

'Right, Julius.'

'So, gentlemen. "Travel and Travellers". The title of our series. Do we make a distinction, Sam Webster, between being a traveller and being a tourist?'

'I think we do, Julius, yes. A tourist buys a package which takes him to a chosen destination, shelters and feeds him there, then brings him back again. By and large, of course, with some variation. But travellers are different, and more complex, I think, in that they are impelled to travel for many kinds of reason, although adventure, the sense of adventure comes into it very strongly.'

'Adventure. Involving risk and danger? Nigel?'

'Often but not necessarily, I would say, yes. For instance, I consider myself to have travelled as a traveller and not just because my academic work took me into a tiny, obscure African tribe. I went in the first instance out of... curiosity, I suppose, not for risk and danger. Because anyone less dangerous than my M'bhutu you could hardly imagine. My first impression of their day, for instance, was largely of them lolling about, as it appeared to me, making jokes that weren't very funny. They'd never seen a blue-eyed man before and every now and then one of them would come up to me, look me over and go off into fits of laughter!'

'You were the novelty of the month, were you?'

'I was, but not in the sense you imply, Julius. Because what it took me quite some time to appreciate was that the laughter was not actually about amusement or derision or anything like that but rather the expression of a kind of... appreciative incredulity. And in fact the name they gave me, since they were quite incapable of uttering the words "Nigel Wheatley", meant "godlike". I was "the godlike one". I should add that they do not fear their gods, not at all. On the contrary, they treat them with a kind of... conniving familiarity, like old mates with whom you can share a risqué anecdote. Sorry, this is all a bit of a red herring.'

'A fascinating one, nevertheless. Geoffrey Hayward, any thoughts on curiosity?'

'I wanted to know, so I went to see.'

'Sounds like a quotation.'

'It is. From the Greek historian Herodotus.'

'Who travelled extensively in the ancient world, did he not, to gather material for his *Histories*?'

'He did, yes.'

'So, Geoff. Curiosity?'

'Certainly, for me curiosity plays the same part in the business of travel as it seems to do for Nigel. I agree absolutely with what has been said so far, Julius. I suppose one could imagine that there may well be people around for whom risk or danger may be more imperative, but they are far more likely, it seems to me, to be soldiers or mountaineers or potholers or something. For me, certainly, curiosity is by far the strongest impulse—'

'Precisely because—'

'Yes, Sam Webster?'

'Sorry, Geoff.'

'No, no. Do go on, Sam.'

'Thank you. Precisely because what curiosity is about is a fascination for what is strange, the urge to investigate strangeness, the... strange significance, for instance, of the M'bhutu laughter. Nice title there, incidentally, Nigel, don't you think?'

'M'bhutu Laughter? I do actually, yes, Sam. But you can't have it!'

'Ha! ha! ha!'

'No, no, Nigel. I wouldn't dream of pirating your words! No, what I was wondering was whether, once you had become more familiar with your M'bhutu, the lolling about and the apparently unfunny jokes didn't come to make more sense?'

'You're absolutely right, Sam. Of course they did.'

'Once you'd acquired something of the language?'

'That primarily I suppose, yes, Julius.'

'Which implies a number of other things, doesn't it?'

'Indeed, Geoff.'

'Such as?'

'Such as... Expressive reactions, non-verbal reactions that is, to things that happen which make meaning evident, if you see what I mean.'

'You mean, gestures and things?'

'Well, one needs to be a bit careful on that one. What may be perfectly acceptable in one culture may be quite horrendously not in another. Any linguist has tales to tell of appalling gaffes that turn the blood to water fifty years after they happened. Gesture is even more dangerous ground, it seems to me, than language.'

'Yes, gentlemen. Let's return to language, if we may. Travellers tend to be linguists, do they? Sam?'

'Geoff is. Geoff speaks any number of weird languages—'

'Lappish isn't weird—'

'Just slightly out of the way, you might say?'

'I suppose I must allow that, Julius. From our vantage point I suppose it must seem so, certainly. But it's only weird until it becomes familiar. I recall vividly a man at Cambridge saying in a lecture that beneath the most outlandish manifestations of difference there is always a common humanity to be found. That was one of those notions that determine the course of a life subsequently, as it did mine, and I know it to be true.'

'Sam?'

'One can also, I think, use the experience of difference, and I suppose I am talking about cultural difference, though conditions of living come into this as well, to find out things about oneself and about life as one has grown up to live it at home. There are lots of examples of this in the literature of travel, as I'm sure you know, Julius, of people who have deliberately distanced themselves to find a new perspective on things we tend to take for granted. And there are elaborate ways of doing this. Oliver Goldsmith's Chinaman is a case in point—'

'Could you elaborate on that one, Sam? Quickly, please.'

'Goldsmith, in the eighteenth century, wrote a book entitled *The Chinese Letters* which purported to be correspondence from a diplomatic representative in London to a friend in Peking, in which he described and commented upon the fashionable social life of a Western metropolis.'

'That's a very literary way of going about it. A writer's trick. Artifice.'

'True, Nigel. Going to see, like Herodotus, and making comparisons is the more usual way of doing it. Pity Herodotus never met my nomads, actually.'

'Terrific! Geoffrey Hayward, thank you very much. And thank you, Sam Webster and Nigel Wheatley, whose films will be showing on this channel very shortly in our new series, "Travel and Travellers". Watch out then, viewers, for the "Case of the Vanishing Colonel" – that's Nigel Wheatley's – "Coming across Crocodiles" from Sam Webster, and "Travels in Iceland" from Geoffrey Hayward…'

★

Dear Doctor and Mrs Barraclough,

Here at last, as I promised, is the latest I have to tell you on Eleanor Tew.

It transpired that, although there was apparently nothing in the archive at Clough, the search carried out there had overlooked the fact that there existed a further cache of material, which had been stored elsewhere for the college, thanks to an offer from another college of space in a neighbouring house on the edge of Newnham village.

This was duly communicated to me, once she had been made aware of it, by the young historian, Doctor Rainsford, who had been very helpful over the initial, abortive search which we undertook together at Clough in January.

Duly then, I returned to Cambridge where this lady and I made a further search, this time of the attic at Newnham Lodge; we discovered a box of material filed under the name of Miss Tew which included a journal, leather-bound and somewhat battered and water-stained, which, with a joint effort, we were to decipher and interpret. I should add that our interpretations of certain aspects of this fascinating, often very moving and certainly very extraordinary text were not invariably in agreement. I shall shortly be in a position to consider the possibility of a novel based on the story of Miss Tew: it seems to me that hers is a story which ought to be well worth the telling, provided it is appropriately written. Being the novelist I am, I shall quite simply invent fiction to make good what is missing from the diary. I am sure you can imagine what my feelings were when we at last opened the volume, to see in front of us that same gracious, cursive Victorian script as appears in the inscription to Anna Rowlandson in your copy of the Bavarian Journal.

The journal tells the remarkable story of a life led amongst the nomads of the Bakhtiari Mountains of south-west Persia, continuing for several years beyond the 'disappearance', which, it seems, was a voluntary severing of links with the Western world in the interest of a more complete identification with the nomads, 'her dear friends', of whom Miss Tew claimed to have become one. Those passages of the journal in which reference is made to the character of the mountainous, wild country over which they wander, these ancient tribes, with their flocks, are frequently of great literary beauty; they are, at the same time, infused with a sense of celebration, of intense imaginative delight at the wonder, the sheer mystery and strange, strange beauty of it all. As regards the nomadic people whom she so clearly loved and with whom she chose, at such cost, to identify, there is, regretfully, little said. From what I had told her of the Bavarian Journal, *Doctor Rainsford, a somewhat formidable young woman of extraordinary intellectual and scholarly perspicacity, maintained that this deliberate withholding of references to anything of a private nature was only in keeping with the essentially private nature of Eleanor herself, as well as being something entirely in keeping with the reticence of that culture, the Victorian, in which she had grown up, despite the many freedoms of the Tew ethos, which equally she must have enjoyed from a father such as hers. Which brings me to another important consideration. What kind of imperatives, one wonders, could have impelled her to dissociate herself so completely from a father such as Theophilus Tew, to whom she had been so devoted? This is explained by the journal in two ways, for, in the briefest of passing references, Miss Tew signals the fact of her motherhood, that she had given birth to Bakhtiari male children – a matter of great importance, clearly, to the nomadic way of life, since it is on the strength of the men that the survival of the flocks which constitute the wealth and estate of the tribesfolk depend. Nothing could have been calculated to invest her with greater significance as a woman of the tribe than that she should have achieved this. Miss Rainsford surmised, quite without any justification at the level of historical fact, that, since there was a history of twins in the Tew family, it might be considered to have been not unlikely that... Of a nomad lover, of the father of her children she makes no mention. He must remain, in the words of my donnish companion, and not inappropriately in my view, 'a shadowy male figure silhouetted in the doorway of a tent at dusk'. One further consideration gives credence to this view: this is the fact that Miss Tew writes with such obvious admiration of 'the splendid men' of the tribe.*

The second point to be made in the matter of any attempt to account for the 'untimely disappearance' of this exceptional lady is altogether a sadder one.

At the time of the concluding entries – concluding to all intents and purposes although the journal remains uncompleted – Miss Tew makes mention of her own imminent demise from a 'wasting sickness'. And indeed, the journal ends as her strength fails her, but not before she has noted the arrangements she has planned to have it conveyed into the hands of a diplomatic representative of Her Majesty, and thence to the Principal of Clough Hall, Cambridge, where it was to remain unread for a period of fifty years. She determined on this course of action in order that her surviving relatives might be spared such pain as the news of her survival and subsequent terminal illness might have caused them. As all this is, then, one cannot but grieve for what must have been the pain of the later years of Theophilus Tew. And the case becomes only the more poignant when one imagines how he would have exulted, most likely, being the man he was, in the exceptional destiny of his beloved daughter.

It is a remarkable and moving story which has lain, since 1936, when the fifty year prohibition came to an end, forgotten and neglected amongst the effects of the college, although someone at some time must have assembled and boxed the Tew materials in that nondescript brown package. There's another story there...

When I have decided how I may make responsible use of all this in the fiction whose precise character is yet to be determined, I shall refer the matter to you again. In the meantime, my thanks once again, Doctor Barraclough, for that happy hunch of yours which led me to this discovery...

Chapter Four

Sam had decided to travel out to Venice by train, as Jacquetta would be doing the same thing from Aix-en-Provence. The idea of their converging in similar style upon a point had about it the kind of whimsical appeal for which he was in the mood, now that the Kingsley film was well and truly completed and he was effectively between jobs. Besides, he was apprehensive and wanted time to reflect. Travel by train would help: one could sit and stare out at changing landscapes and architectures and ponder things. And, indeed, how many countless travellers and hopeful, putative lovers must have gone this way before? Sam thought of trains of years gone by – of the Blue Train, of the Orient Express, of trains leaving London from Blackfriars for Hamburg, Berlin, Warsaw, Smolensk. To watch landscapes change was to experience an enrichment of the business of travel which no rapid flight through the anonymity of cloud or dark could ever equal. Trains were for lovers. Sam imagined the moment of their meeting, their rendezvous at a modest *pensione* on the Zattere.

Outside, now, there was a view of mountains, snow-capped and massive. Bavaria. The occasional onion-domed church showed up, a tiny, metallic glitter against the colossal, unchanging, natural configurations of rock. The *Bavarian Journal*. Sam thought briefly of two venturesome young Victorian ladies trudging their way by forest and lake, engaged as ever in earnest discourse. The delight of it was without compare. The notion of a new story, a new idea to be worked upon, the knowledge that it was there and that he would inevitably write it and bring it to some kind of eventual completion was a vital, sustaining thing. There had been, there *were* writers who had discarded virtually every other consideration in life to give themselves more fully to the pursuit of this solitary, intense, incomparable act.

And Jacquetta Rainsford? She would be leaving shortly, leaving now, making her early morning way down the Cours Mirabeau... How long had they got, Sam wondered. What inscrutable chemistry, what elective affinities would determine the course of their affair? The solitary working life was one to which he had long since accommodated his ways and inclinations, but bed with a strapping young enthusiast brought its own sense of renewal, which was instantaneous...

*

The hotel room he had taken looked out onto a narrow waterway leading off the Zattere and away into the heart of the city in the direction of the Grand Canal itself. On previous occasions, whether alone or accompanied, Sam had sat on the tiny balcony overlooking the water to watch the timeless comings and goings of the city, the odd gondola, the occasional commercial barge, the inevitable cats that stalked the walkways before the burning heat of the Venetian sun drove them into the shade.

Drowsily now, in the sun-hazed dreaminess of afternoon, he recalled the feel of her against him, the softness, the sand-scented warmth of her hair, the wonderful glint of conniving mischief twinkling from brown eyes alight with high intelligence. And with the sensuous reminiscence, something more, even more precious – the mutual thing, the notion of something between them that was both willed and reciprocal, the sense of being implicated together, of no longer being entirely solitary. And at the back of his mind, more distant but at one with his sense of her, there was also the recollection of a wild, gorgeous, phantom landscape with mountains, with figures moving laboriously over it, a dream vision of high and lonely places.

Across the room the door latch clicked.

'Eleanor?' he heard himself say, the syllables barely voiced.

Then, turning towards the sound, he had had a brief glimpse through the open window of the view down the little canal, with the perfect arc, to scale, of an exquisite bridge, a receding perspective of buildings characteristically lurching at angles, light – mellowing now – on water and, further away, a cluster of fantastical chimney pots. The door opened.

'Hello, Sam,' said Jacquetta Rainsford.

'Hello, darling,' said Sam.

Then he moved across to her and she walked into his arms, and for one quite timeless moment their embrace was full of delight.